Jan 1996

to the Meles —

The most wonderful family
I know.

Debby

Cross a Dark Bridge

A Novel

by

Deborah Churchman

Ariadne Press
Rockville, Maryland

Copyright © Deborah Churchman 1996

Library of Congress Cataloging-in-Publication Data
Churchman, Deborah.
    Cross a dark bridge: a novel / by Deborah Churchman.
       p.   cm.
    ISBN 0-918056-08-X
    1. Married people—Eastern Shore (Md. and Va.)—Fiction.
2. Multiple personality—Fiction. 3. Twins—Fiction. I. Title.
PS3553.H863C76   1996
813'.54—dc20   95-34124
                                                                     CIP

Jacket design: Leslie Murray
Typesetting: Barbara Shaw

Ariadne Press
4817 Tallahassee Ave.
Rockville, Maryland
20853

for John, Landes, and all those that live inside

Chapter 1

November, 1989

MR. DEETERS

The first time I saw Gilead my wife was in November of 1989. She was tilted against an Amoco station that stood spitting distance from the Annapolis side of the Chesapeake Bay Bridge. Her body made a strange sort of flying buttress there against the wall. With her thin arms wrapped around her, nothing was left to break the sheer linear design of the girl. Every part—the triangles of sandy hair at her temples and forehead, the flat, almost Asiatic nose, the long body rising like an arrow from sandaled feet—pointed directly to her eyes. The black hole eyes of a ghost. My ghost.

Everything else about her irritated me. Her Peter Pan body seemed pinioned in perpetual immaturity. Too old to be a girl, it was clear she'd chosen not to be a woman. Just looking at her aged me. And frightened me. There was something not right about her, something powerful and disabling. It was as if with one false step, she could cause the whole of reality to suddenly become unlinked, one molecule at a time.

And then there was her family. Impossible. Impossible!

But the eyes I recognized instantly, with that shock you feel gazing at the night sky and finding yourself suddenly confronted with the inescapable notion of eternity. They were the eyes of the one I had come to think of as the Other—my twin brother, dead already these 36 years. I saw them only in dreams; they accused me, pleaded with me. I thought I could keep them safely there under the weight of darkness. Now they were here, in front of me. I knew them. Looking at them, I saw that the eyes knew me as well. Me—Nathan Deeters.

GILEAD

We were stopped at a gas station. I don't know why. There had been loops and blanks the whole way. People would tell me where we were, what day. "Tuesday," I'd say, telling myself over and over. "Pennsylvania." And then it would be Wednesday, and somewhere else. I've never understood time; it shakes, like light bouncing through fun-house mirrors.

My sister's face is like a mirror. Mother says it's because we're twins. I look at that to see myself. I never know how to be, what to feel. Everything in front of me looks random, bouncy, elusive. I can't grasp it. But my sister Missy's face tells me what's important, what to look at.

So I looked at Missy. And then, because her eyes told me to, I looked at him. Nathan Deeters.

MR. DEETERS

I was picking up my car at Mike's Amoco, an hour away from my home in Cambridge—a fact that slammed me at once against her difficult family. I would have found her in any case; the gods are relentless that way. As it was, our beginning nearly drowned in the odorousness of that family, a kind of cat-spray stink from which I've never quite recovered.

"Hey, Nate," said Mike, owner of the station and the only man on the Eastern shore I'd trust with my Volvo. I almost have to sneak it over there behind the back of all my potential gas station-owner customers at home. But it's worth it; Mike is a genius. "I'se hoping you'd stop by soon," he was telling me. "Wonder if you might help these folks out," he said, pointing to the vast terrain of Grasons—the flunky son slinking around the back of their battered red VW bus with its Ohio plates, the portly sister whose eyes held a dissonant echo of the Other, the fusty, fat mother in a fraying pink coat and wrinkled scarf. And Gilead, holding up the reality of the gas station with her lithe, ethereal body. "That ol' bus of theirs done broke down for a spell—

can't get the part till Tuesday. And now they gotta get to Easton to visit Miz Grason's sister—Claudia Bunting, mebbe you know her?" he asked.

"The Post Office widow," I replied without thinking. That knowledge of their destination fed me right into the family's clutches; now I was stuck.

"Oh, exactly, exactly!" cried Missy, eyes crevassing into a Gotcha! smile. "Isn't it wonderful, Mama?" she said, pushing her sentence in the general direction of frayed pinkness. "This gentleman even knows Auntie! Oh, sir, you are a true knight to these damsels in distress. Isn't he, Mama?" The thing called Mama stared with tiny pig eyes, giving me a look of genial puzzlement.

I'd been taken without a battle. Belatedly, I felt the troops rising within me. "I'm not sure I could fit you all in my. . . ."

"Oh, don't worry about a thing, sir," Missy said definitively. "We Grasons are accustomed to traveling in European vehicles. We'll simply put Gilly on Freddy's lap, and Mama and I will be most comfortable in your back seat. I see your car has a trunk; thank goodness. So many cars are doing without these days; such a loss, I think, don't you? Don't worry, we are traveling light—absolute minimum baggage. Freddy!" she screeched as I was beginning to garner my excuses. "Bring the bags!"

Missy strode directly to her brother's side to jackhammer her request. Then, as her daughter shifted from her limited vision, the pink mother turned her rouged face to me. "Missy's the strong twin," she said, indicating the daughter with weight plunging toward her brother. "Gilead's the shy twin," she explained.

I turned to gaze at the Other, leaning against the gas station wall. "So they're twins?" I asked. Something in me knew that already, and was strangely comforted by the report.

The fat, flighty head bobbed chaotically. "Identical," she said, and giggled. "Hard to believe, huh?"

"I think I can see some resemblance," I began.

"I'm so sorry about this," the mother interrupted. To my horror, she started to cry, with round, blubbering tears dripping from her eyes. "It's the bridge, of course," she said.

"Pardon me?" I asked. The statement buzzed about me like a fly in the kitchen, distracting me from the more urgent task of scrolling through my mind for an unanswerable excuse. No, I thought, I won't have this dreadful family in my car.

"That terrible bridge," she said, pointing in the direction of the Bay. There the bridge rose like a masterful spider's web, hugging the two shores. "Our bus could sense it, I'm sure," she said. "That's why it broke down here—for protection. Protection from the bridge."

"Ah, I see," I lied; rarely have I felt this blind. "So you believe the bridge has, um, powers?"

"It's a web," she said. "I've had nightmares about it for years. Sometimes I can skirt the edges and make the link back to my family. But eventually, I get caught. We all get caught by the bridge."

Now I knew for certain this sought-after assistance of mine simply could not be rendered. I have always had a fear of the mad, even stronger than my fear of aggressive women. This family had both, along with a male whose greasy arms were bound to stain my upholstery irreparably. The fact that it also had Gilead did nothing to dissuade me. I carefully positioned myself so that I couldn't see Gilead's eyes, and began. "Madam, I fear I cannot take you to your sister's," I said. "I won't be returning there for several hours myself. Some errands in Annapolis," I said, pointing vaguely in the opposite direction of her source of nightmares.

I sensed the body of the Other behind me. She had left her role of holding up the gas station wall, and moved lightly, like mist, to my side. I looked down, and saw her tentative smile. Her arm moved in slow motion toward mine, like a feather ruffled upward by the wind. Her hand touched me. It touched me and I felt a deep, erotic shock. I pulled back involuntarily, shuddering with the intensity of that feeling. I had a sudden, irrational sense of being in the presence of something unearthly—some obscure goddess, perhaps, or a demon whose name has long been erased from the memory of mankind. But when I looked, I saw only a frightened girl. I wondered at the fundamental terror rimming her eyes. She spoke.

"Mother speaks on the edges of language," she said in a faint voice.

I looked directly at her; her eyes lowered quickly. I waited for more explanation; none was forthcoming.

I can't explain my reaction to her. I'm a grocery store manager; the world I know has weight and size and three firm dimensions. Things do not blur at the edges of my world; they are neatly cut and wrapped. Yet I had lately come to wonder about those edges. Perhaps it was the dreams, recurring, recurring. Perhaps I had gone a little mad from dreaming, hearing the voice that called from death.

"And you?" I asked, as gently as I could. For she was like a bird that would come to my hand only, I thought, if I held very still. "Do you speak on the edges of language?"

She lifted those haunted eyes to meet mine, flicked them over my face. I felt caressed. "I am the other part," she said in small print voice. "I am the silent half of language."

GILEAD

When I looked at him, I saw something tall with a clear, firm shape. The shape was like a many-grooved cookie cutter. I could see he'd been stamped out by someone else, something else. But the firmness, the clarity of that impressed shape was starting to decay from within. The decay made him a little blurry, I think. It fuzzed over his rigid edges and gentled him.

I liked him.

As I walked closer, I could see he was becoming upset with Mama. Still that didn't explain what I saw growing within him. It was a yearning, the kind you see in plants left too long in basement corners, with long pale shoots searching frantically for the light. Something in him, some long entombed seed, was starting to yield to the dogmatic command: Grow. Grow.

Chapter 2

November 1989 - April 1990

MISSY

Let's start this whole thing over. I know how Deeters sees things, and he's got it all wrong. I am not Gilead's twin sister. I am a fictional character, the realized gift of my own imagination.

I am the actualized reality of Mathilda on All My Sorrows, which comes on afternoons at two. I used to believe, in my precious, younger life, that I was the actualized reality of Clarissa on Day's Turnings, which comes on at the same time. But I realized through the grace of the Almighty and the irritating reception of Channel 5 that I belonged on All My Sorrows; that was Me. Oh, I mightn't be as thin as Mathilda, but they get nothing but anorexic actresses to play these parts. That Mathilda is a real person in a fictional part; I am a fictional person in a real life.

Some facts, of course, Deeters probably has right; it's the tone that's all wrong. Take the part about the bridge: I'll bet he simply says we met near the bridge. Ha! That first meeting was the fault, the very creation, of the Bay Bridge.

The bridge is an umpteen-mile, oh-so-long affair that spans the Chesapeake Bay. It looks, to be frank, like something designed by deranged engineers playing with erector sets. While for many—perhaps millions—of people the bridge represents a gateway between two shores, for us it was a wall. It may be fairer and clearer to call it The Wall.

We had been urging mother to make this journey to Auntie's for quite some time—two years, in fact, since the day Gilead and I graduated from high school. After father's unfortunate demise, the plot had twisted downward. That dreadful man from the insurance company had refused to pay, and father's pension barely covered costs. Did not, in fact, cover costs. The rental agent was so unpleasant, though we tried to pay something each month, and mother always baked for him. Mother's useful hints, published in those ladies' magazines she so enjoys, weren't truly profit-makers. Freddy, our older brother, said they covered the cost of the magazines, barely.

Not that Freddy was making any effort to boost the family income. True, he did take on the odd occasional mechanical job—Freddy is good with engines and all that—but it hardly put bread on the table. I was in charge of the family's plotline, which left me no time to earn an income. And Gilly of course was not capable at that stage of, well…Gilly was, as they say on the talk shows, in a difficult place. Another good reason to move.

The obvious plot solution was to go to the one relative with a sustainable income, Aunt Claudia. This lighthouse of the family had stayed behind in Cambridge, Maryland, marrying a postal worker who rose to head up that city's center, while Mother married father and followed his job. Claudia was still there, widowed now but living in the lap of pensioned luxury.

I set about steering the plot toward Aunt Claudia, which was a lot more difficult than you might imagine. But not, as you may be thinking, for reasons of false pride. A family smitten by tragedy like ours needs the cushion of mercy; it would be selfish on our part to refrain from receiving our family's solace and outpourings of love.

Well, perhaps outpourings isn't quite the right word. Aunt Claudia's letter in response to mine was a tad chilly and discouraging. But I felt that her protests of economic deprivation and lack of space were exaggerated, and urged mother to read between the lines for the glints of sisterly love, care, and affection to be found therein.

Also there was no other choice. Mother's brother is a rambler with no roof to call his own. And father's family turned their back on us, blaming us for the death. (To be fair, they'd already turned their noses up at mother by the time Freddy was born, and didn't even acknowledge Gilly's and my birth.)

Mother agreed to cast herself on Aunt Claudia's care, but found hundreds of reasons to delay the casting. The last reason— probably the bottom reason—was the bridge. Mother had her fortune done when she was a teenager (the first of several hundred such episodes) and was told she would die plunging from a high place. She has since replaced that statement in her mind with an idee fixe that she will die falling from the Bay Bridge.

Reason doesn't touch such fears. Neither does manipulation. What finally moved her was a combination of promises to check the VW bus thoroughly before attempting the crossing of the Bay and to shelter her in the back of the bus while the journey was made. That and the eviction notice tacked alarmingly on the front door of our suburban Cinncinnati shelter.

But the bus broke down, just past Annapolis. Enter Nathan Deeters, our man to the rescue. I observed him carefully, and thought about him a great deal over the next few months.

FREDDY

Talk about your set-ups! Poor old Deeters never had a chance. I could see him over by the station looking cornered, if that's possible in a land this flat. But I was still trying to juggernaut the engine into going, running the risk of burning the damn thing out in the process, when Missy started screeching for the luggage.

Even Gilly was in on trying to con this guy into a ride. Why, I'll never know. Gilly kind of tunes in and out, especially on trips. Mother had been blubbering all morning about having to face that bridge, so I figured Gilly would definitely be on the Tune Out cycle. Instead, Our Lady of Perpetual Fear (that's what I call her) was edging over to this guy's Volvo.

So I followed. Hell, *I* didn't care how we got to Cambridge; I just wanted this thing to be over with. Mother was another story, of course. She ducked into the back seat, threw her head onto Missy's lap back there, and kept up a steady moan that rose and fell in between Missy's non-stop chatter.

And of course Missy had to tell this guy every living detail of our lives, how Mother grew up on the Eastern shore, who she married, how much older I was than the twins, all about their high school graduation, the fact that father was dead and we were moving back "home," if you can call a place where you've never lived "home," etc. Gilly sat on my lap in the front seat during all of this, gazing out the window. She'd started to shake almost as soon as she sat down. I was hoping the guy wouldn't notice, but he did.

"Are you cold?" he asked, reaching for the heater and punching buttons. Gilly was too out of it by then to answer; I told him she was fine. "But she's shaking," he said. "Perhaps there's a sweater in the luggage that she could put on?"

"She's just fine," I told him again. What was he, deaf?

"Then why isn't she talking?" he asked.

"Oh, Gilly never talks," Missy explained. There. It was out.

That slowed the guy's mouth down, I noticed. I snuck a quick peek at him, but saw him staring intently over the wheel, going up the bridge. It wasn't until he started passing a truck somewhere near the middle of the bridge, with mother's moans getting louder and louder, that he asked, out of the blue, "not even on the telephone?"

That's when I knew Gilly had him, sure as she'd stuck a pin in him and slapped on a label: Mine. Missy knew it too—I could tell by the way she was breathing, with quick little sucks of air. Mother had no idea, of course; she was too busy having The Worst Experience of Her Life, as she called it. But I'll tell you something strange: Gilly didn't know it either. Gilly never had any idea what effect she had on people. She just did whatever Missy told her to do.

MISSY

One night as I was squirreled away in my little room, writing my family's destiny, I had one of those flashes of insight great writers hold so dear. I saw Mr. Deeters as our way out of the cliffhanger position I'd written us into in this godforsaken corner of the universe. Mr. Deeters—store owner with a steady income and a Volvo, man with a mousetrap-shaped grasp of figures, upright member of the Episcopal Church, respected bachelor of the town. A man who commanded such awe, even my mother paid cash at his store. Who better to relieve us of the tedious necessity of making a living?

Working with only the characters available to me, I saw swiftly that Gilead was the best choice to reach this protective sanctuary of Mr. Deeters. Our mother is somewhat closer to his age, of course, but mother, whose diets have been failing lately and who suffers from what the 19th century anyway clearly understood as fragile nerves, would be too winded to make the stretch. Our aunt, with her incessant carping over what a burden we are to her, was totally unsuitable; I'm seriously considering writing her out of this novel. And besides, she'd had years to attract him and had never so much as made his social aquaintance. Also, she's even older than mother. Men are sensitive about being seen with mature women.

I could have written myself in for the part, but Mr. Deeters treats me with a teasing disdain because of a simple mix-up over my name. When we first met under those true knight-errant circumstances, I was just reaching enlightenment over my identity as Mathilda instead of Clarissa. But because the understanding was not fully clarified in my mind, I gave him both names in the course of our initial conversation. And of course Freddy would persist in calling me Missy, whereas Mother calls me Michelle, the name she says she authored when I was born. That's in your novel, I told her. I'm Mathilda in mine.

Gilead, of course, said almost nothing, an attribute Mr. Deeters found appealing. A man of Mr. Deeters' character runs a Skinnearean maze of figures and orders all day long; the quality of silence speaks directly to his heart.

And so, I arranged a courtship.

MR. DEETERS

And so I began trying to court this elusive girl. The process pushed me immediately beyond my limits; it seemed to call for more techniques than I had ever developed in my small life. I knew at once that it would do no good to reach out and grasp her; nothing that ethereal can be held for long. Here is what I did instead: I opened a door into myself, leading directly to the cavernous hole left by my twin, and invited her in. I am a private person by nature; opening the hole was a painful and difficult process. And I had only hope and no real expectations that she would step inside. At first, she left each time after looking into the open doorway, sending me into painful bouts of doubt and self-recrimination. And as I felt her going deeper into virgin territory, I had to fight off the terror all men have of being known by a woman; fight off the obsessional yearning to possess that knowledge. For I know that she knows me. And as I came to know her—Gilead the twin, Gilead the otherworldly—I became more and more convinced that she was the link I needed to reunite me with the twin of my soul.

Even just meeting up with Gilead was difficult, to say the least. That family made something as simple as the telephone impossible. For the family—and I'm sure it's the family—has made my darling practically mute. Except for that one conversation we had at the gas station, Gilly has almost never spoken to me. When she does, her words are, at best, spare.

Her twin sister Missy, nattering at me during that first, execrable drive with her family, explained Gilead's aversion to talking. "Not even on the telephone?" I asked, wondering frantically how I'd make contact with this girl in the future.

"Oh, particularly not the telephone. Gilead never talks on the telephone," her sister said from the back seat, where she and her mother sat, lowering the car's body with their combined, phenomenal weight. Not to mention the family's hideous and plentiful luggage. The back end has never been the same.

If the telephone was out of the question, dropping by the house was even more unfeasible. I wasn't on social terms with her aunt—I was the owner of a grocery store where she rarely shopped. I considered switching to the aunt's Baptist church on the assumption that the whole family would be there, but quickly noticed that they stayed home during their aunt's Sunday observances. Then a miracle happened: Gilead started showing up at my store with some dim list written by her dim-minded sister.

The bird had come to my feeder.

MISSY

I sent Gilead to Mr. Deeters' store with tidy lists and crisp dollars I'd obtained at the bank, exchanging the torturously folded ones squatting in mother's purse or shrouded beneath auntie's hankies and gloves. I saw to it that Gilly left for the store looking her best. Gilead has mother's beauty without its Rubenesque quality; with some deft tailoring on my part, she presents quite a pretty picture with her sandy hair and elegant legs.

Then there are those haunted eyes. Frankly, I find them rather irritating. Oh, the heart yearns for her, Our Lady of Perpetual Fear (to turn Freddy's phrase), but it does rather get on one's nerves, coming out of the powder room or up from the pantry, to be greeted by someone whose eyes tell of meeting with monsters too hideous to be described. "For pity's sake, Gilly, it's just me," I tell her over and over (and over), but it doesn't stop. It just gets wearying.

I perceived, however, that a man of Mr. Deeters' experience would appreciate my sister's tentative nature. Catering all day to cow-like customers, sacred and otherwise, is not good for a man, and I could see that the obsequious face imposed on Mr. Deeters did not fit well. How much better it would be for him to exert power, to take command. Gilly, of course, wraps what power she has in tiny birthday-party packages, giving them out practically on the streetcorner to any passerby. A woman made to be possessed by any man with a thumb and middle finger still intact. (In fact, we'd had some trouble with that just prior to father's death.)

I saw to it that Mr. Deeters would have ample opportunity to feed on this quality of Gilly's by deliberately making her shopping lists obscure—detergent instead of Tide, dinner vegetables unnamed. You are simply to hand this list to Mr. Deeters, I told my sister firmly; he will know what's best. Then I imagined the conversation, if one can call it that, Gilly being practically mute, between the wise elder and his fragile customer. Green beans look good, Miz Grason, you like a pound today? Quiet nodding with demure eyes. Got a good sale on the 5-lb. box of All, can you cover it? Furtive counting on Gilly's part; trusting nod.

The plan took some adjusting at first; all good plans do. Gilly turned up three times in a row with expensive brands we'd never heard of. Mother was all for going back and giving Mr. Deeters a piece of her mind, such as it is, but I stopped it with a fainting spell. This is my most effective means of dealing with mother; I use it with considerable restraint, when you think of how often it's needed—no more than once or twice a week. Mother begins her day by reading her astrology column and throwing the Tarot; my fainting, followed by a trance-like state in which I send her advice from the Great Beyond, seems a natural extension. Freddy was upset the first few times I tried this, calling me all manner of names and making it quite difficult for mother to concentrate on the sybilline advice. But Auntie was simply enthralled to see it. Asked all kinds of questions. Perhaps I will keep her in my novel.

Anywho (an endearing phrase of Mathilda's, don't you think?), the trance advice sent Gilead, not mother, back to confront Mr. Deeters, something she was pathetically slow about doing. Nearly all her trips to the store could be called languid, a fact which first encouraged me, as I thought it signalled some backroom flexing of Mr. Deeters' command muscles. But Gilead had simply found a slower and more tortuous route to and from the store, avoiding the sidewalk stares of residents by poking along the river.

GILEAD

We were living someplace different now, with an aunt I'd never met. I shared a room with Missy and mother, but the family never let me stay there. I had to get up in the morning, change my clothes, make my bed. Some days it's all I can do to manage the buttons; the whole process of wrapping myself against the day seems overwhelming, and I go blank.

That's not all. Missy made me go to the store. Alone. Freddy volunteered to do the shopping the first time she commanded this, but Missy said no, Gilly must do it. I watched her mirror eyes. Light struck them, reflecting back at me with intense heat. I saw I must move.

The man was at the store. I thought he must have forgotten that we'd met. It made me blush just to look at him. But he hadn't forgotten—he even called me by my name. His voice is gentle.

I could see the thing inside him still trying to grow, desperate to escape the rigid boundaries of his shape. Some other part deeper inside was starting to crumble. I asked him about it, standing at the counter as he piled Missy's needs into a sack. "Have you been having a lot of dreams lately?" I said. He stopped and stared at me. People do that a lot. I shouldn't speak, I know—it always hurts people.

But then he said, Yes. Just that—Yes. And then, How did you know.

"Because I can see you," I said. I saw that I'd frightened him with my words, my corrosive words. I was afraid for him. I was afraid for myself. I grabbed the sack as soon as he was finished, counted out the money as fast as I could, and left.

MISSY

I'm sorry to say that the courtship proceeded at the same pace, despite frequent efforts to speed it up—planting Gilead next to Mr. Deeters in the bank line, walking Gilead past the store evenings at 8:37 when Mr. Deeters locked up, and so on. The thing that finally broke the ice was a casual mention by Gilly that Mr. Deeters went to the library on Thursdays. By leaning on the librarian (who goes to Auntie's church), I was able to determine a few authors Mr. Deeters seemed to favor there in the past, and send Gilly to the library at 1:30 on Thursday afternoons to request them.

MR. DEETERS

I tried to impress upon Gilead the genuine joy I had at seeing her in my store (whenever the other customers would allow it). But it wouldn't do to overwhelm her with gregarious chatter; I could see that at once. And she always seemed distracted and uncomfortable in the store, gathering her few things, paying with strangely crisp dollar bills, and leaving as quickly as possible.

I found that I measured my days by whether or not Gilly stopped by. That made for many dark days, and a few punctuated by a frustrated sense of incompleteness. But I could see that I held her interest. She started to tell me things about myself—little hints. The strange part is that they were all things I barely knew myself—interior musings I had in half-wakened moments. She'd ask me about my dreams, or suggest that something was haunting me. But sometimes she noticed more practical things. She told me that my elbow was hurting, for instance—something I'd only become aware of that morning. Another time she told me the reason my fingers were fumbling was something slightly strained in my shoulder. I asked her how she knew these things; she said she could see that they were true. I tried to look her directly in the eye, wondering if I'd see myself mirrored there. But she always looked downward; left too soon.

I needed to see her outside the context of my employment, I felt. I was immensely curious about these strange insights of hers. Then one day, I saw her carrying a book. I seized the opportunity.

"May I see what you're reading?" I said, ignoring the growing line behind her.

She turned the title toward me. It was *The Prince of Tides*, by some author I'd never heard of. However, it was a library book. "Wonderful library we have here, isn't it?" Mrs. Hatch began piling her cans of soup on the counter beside Gilead's purchases; I bagged Gilly's items, but slowly.

Gilead nodded at my statement. It was true; she never spoke when a gesture or a glance would suffice.

"I go to the library every Thursday when I have some help at the store," I told her. "At 1:30, after I've finished here." She gave no evidence of having heard, gathered her bagged groceries, and left me wondering what sort of fool I was turning into.

But the information had taken hold, apparently, for I found her at the check-in line at our library the following Thursday, where I'd gone to request a copy of *The Prince of Tides*. She'd brought the book back, along with the family's eclectic supply of mysteries, occult books, diets, religious tomes, and novels by Victor Hugo and Mark Twain. "Ah, Miss Grason, let me, uh, help you," I said, lifting books from her frail-looking arms. My hand inadvertently strayed over one of those limbs; she shrank back, looking at me in terror. I'd come too close to the wild bird; my stomach clutched. "We just need to lift those up here," I said, taking a few books gently from her arms. Stiffly, she lifted the remainder.

"Oh, Mr. Deeters, here's your book!" said Sylvia, our librarian. A good shopper; she always comes in for the half-priced specials, finds them all on the obscure shelves where I've stocked them, and ignores the full-priced displays I've set up attractively near the check-out counters. I found her statement embarrassing, not wanting Gilly to know my plan to read her book and use it as a topic of our bi-weekly conversations.

Truth seemed the best course of action, so I said, "I saw you reading it the other day, and thought it looked good."

She nodded brightly, then opened that tiny mouth. "But the main character is a liar. Remember that."

I was so pleased by this effort of conversation that I nearly let it drop. "I will," I said, watching her back as she wandered toward the stacks. Should I ask her to coffee? I wondered. Should I wait until I'd read the book (it seemed awfully long), when we'd have something to discuss? I find all conversations a bit tricky; having to converse for two would make it necessary to have something solid and complex to discuss, I thought. I checked out the book, and turned toward the door.

And turned back. "Miss Grason," I said when I'd finally gotten her attention in the Mysteries section. "I was wondering if you'd like to go up the street for a cup of coffee?" She stared at me. "Or tea? The hotel serves a brisk cup of tea. And pastries. Do you like pastries?" I wondered if I sounded as much the idiot as I felt. This didn't happen with other women in my life. Being an eligible bachelor at my age made taking out women as simple as gazing in their direction; getting rid of them was the far more difficult task.

Gilead was looking frantically around the stacks. Finally she spoke: "I must get the family's books."

"Of course," I assured her. "Maybe I could help? Perhaps if you showed me the list," I said, referring to the used envelope scribbled with titles in her hand. Obediently, she lifted it to my outstretched arm. In fat pen it enumerated various junk novels, cookbooks, and diets, followed by a familiar name: Brian Moore. I pointed to the author. "He's one of my favorites," I told her. "Shall I pick one out for you?" Without waiting for the hoped-for nod, I strode off in the direction of General Fiction. Then, meeting her back at the checkout counter, I bundled the stamped books under my arms and opened the door for her. Wordlessly, she followed me to the hotel.

And so it went. Over tea that day, and on multiple subsequent afternoons, I discovered that the Silent Half of Language was actually quite wordy on any subject unrelated to her family. It was through these tiny bursts that I was able to peer, however dimly, into the frightened soul of Gilead Grason; all direct conversation about herself or any family members was shut out with silence.

To fill these gaps, I found myself telling her my own story —gradually prying open that door into the hole. I told her of my father's stony sorrow, my mother's desertion, the dreams I'd had for college, the disappointment at having to run the store instead. She interspersed these monologues with questions about my fantasies, my values, my goals—all sorts of things I'd rather not face.

Still, I kept coming back for more.

MISSY

Gilly came home later and later from those Thursday library expeditions, just as I'd hoped. I know exactly what went on. Mr. Deeters, like many store owners in my experience, is a closet teacher, and took it upon himself to advise Gilly on the pros, cons, and messages to be found by a careful reading of each book. Getting Gilly to read the books was no problem—the girl can suck any library dry in less time than it takes to buy the straw—and she apparently began (shyly, of course; that's her style) giving her full agreement to Mr. Deeters' appraisals.

Gilly is big on agreement. She will nod vigorously to any little thing you happen to tell her, face to face. That does not necessarily mean she joins in your conviction; more often than not, it means she'd like to leave the room. But that's the sort of information best left for Mr. Deeters to discover after the wedding. The point was to try and find some form or feeling of Mr. Deeters upon which Gilly could shower her splendid, if shallow, cooperation. The books obviously did just that.

They were stepping right into the roles I was writing for them.

MR. DEETERS

Gilead had a disconcerting habit of treating each of my answers as truth. Many of them—especially in the beginning—were lies that had become so automatic, they'd taken on the aura of truth. It began with the subject of women.

"You aren't married," she observed over her apple crumb pie. The unasked question hung in the air, curiously detached from her, not ominous.

I'd grown to rely on that pie. The first time she ordered it, she picked three bites and gave the rest to me. After that, I found myself looking forward weekly to talking with Gilly and eating two-thirds of a slice of pie. "I suppose I've never found Ms. Right," I answered, wishing she'd hurry up with her third bite. It was a truly delicious crust.

But she was holding me in a steady gaze, so I continued my explanation. She could hold that gaze forever until a complete answer was forthcoming. "I've had friendships with women," I explained as decorously as I could, "but none of them," here I sighed. The sigh had become a ritual part of the explanation, "none has worked out...well."

The gaze disappeared, and she began poking again at the pie. "What did you do to them?" she asked before the third bite popped into her delicate mouth. I'd spent a lot of time fantasizing about that mouth, imagining what it would be like to press myself against those lips.

I'd missed the question. "What did I...?"

"Do to them," she answered between chews.

I left them, I thought. Occasionally one left me—usually as I was on my way out the door. "I'm not sure I understand your question," I said, stalling for time to formulate a more acceptable, yet vague, answer.

"Women are scary," she said, putting down her fork. At last!

"Not to me," I told her. "May I?" I asked, indicating the longed-for pie. As she passed me her plate, I said, "I think women are beautiful people."

She gave me a look that indicated she thought I was lying through my teeth. Which, of course, I was. She gazed out the window, a move which meant that Gilly was done with conversation. It became urgent for me to find an answer; once the gaze out the window started, it became well-nigh impossible for her to find her way back to the here and now. I knew; I'd lost her in Neverland before. "Perhaps I just need the love of a good woman to set me straight," I said quickly. Another automatic lie.

She seemed to go blank for a second, and then glanced at me, giving me a fleck of attention. "And what," she asked, "would you do with a good woman?"

"Probably leave her," I said, thinking of all the perfectly good women I'd left behind before this. I hadn't meant to admit that; I just needed to keep her precarious attention.

She was smiling suddenly, a raw, open smile I'd never seen before. I think the honesty pleased her. Her whole attitude had shifted. Where before she perched delicately on her chair, now she was sprawled over it. She casually unclipped her long hair, which fell luxuriantly onto her shoulders. It gave me a bit of a jolt, to see her looking so sexy and open.

She looked me directly in the eye. "And what would you do with a bad woman?" she asked in a low, warm voice.

I puzzled over that, hoping for as honest an answer as I was capable of. "I'm not sure," I said. "Actually, I don't think a bad woman would be attracted to someone like me. I'm too…"

"Straight?" she asked.

I drew in breath; was that how she saw me? "I suppose you could put it that way," I said evenly.

"Perhaps she'd want to corrupt you," Gilly said.

I chuckled. "I used to fantasize about things like that," I said, thinking back to the frantic, hormone-driven days of my adolescence.

She sucked in air, lowered her head slightly, and asked, "Do you have a lot of sexual fantasies?" In the middle of the hotel, right over the white damask table cloth!

"Well, no, now that I'm older, I mean, I hardly ever…"

"But surely you must have some," she urged.

"Well, I suppose it's only normal for a healthy male to, um…"

"Do you have more than one woman in these fantasies?" she asked.

I didn't like where this was leading at all. Was she testing me to see if I'd gone past the pervert line? "I think about different women at different times, I suppose," I said. How to change this conversation?

"I meant did you ever fantasize about taking more than one woman at a time?" she pursued.

This had gone far enough. "Gilead, I'm very uncomfortable talking about these things with…"

"My father used to fantasize about having sex with two women at the same time," she said.

"Your father!" I practically shouted.

"But I don't think he ever did it. In fact, I'm sure of it. He would have told me," she said. "Don't they serve anything stronger than tea around here?"

◊ ◊ ◊

We got onto the subject of the hump the next week by discussing Thomas Mann and his deformed characters. I told her the automatic lie—a lie I gave not just to women to elicit their sympathy (it always worked), but also to myself, to keep from considering the truth. "I've had some experience with a handicap, as you probably know," I said. This was a probe, actually. Half of Cambridge knew about the deformity, including her aunt. Would she admit to the knowledge?

"So does my brother," she told me. "He couldn't read; mixed up his letters. My sister cured him, though," she said, daintily sipping her tea. "She bought him car manuals. He ate them up."

"I was referring to a, um, growth on my back," I replied.

She lifted her eyes from her usual gaze at the table. "So it's true?" she asked.

"Yes, ah," I said. Good girl; you came clean, I thought. "Your aunt must have told you," I stated.

"She told Missy and me that they called you the hunchback," Gilead said. "But that suddenly after your father died, it was gone. So everyone supposed you'd gotten it taken off."

I smiled a strained smile, meant to underscore my pain. "My years of being the hunchback finally ended," I said quietly. And waited for the effect, confident that I'd finally elicited her sympathy.

She shifted a little in her seat—unusual, for her; Gilly moves as little as she talks—and started swinging her leg. "Did it make you creepy?" she asked in a squeaky voice.

"I beg your pardon?"

"Kids with handicaps tend to creep around, trying to be invisible, learning to hide in plain sight," she said. "Either that, or they become outrageous to distract attention from the deformity. You don't strike me as outrageous," she smiled. Then she leaned over the table and, using her teaspoon, took a bite of her/my pie.

I smiled back, one primate responding to another's facial expression. But her words made me angry. "I don't think of myself as creepy, either," I said.

Gilead looked genuinely puzzled. "So what did it make you do?" she asked.

"I made me hurt," I said, a little too sharply. I looked, expecting a gush of sympathy, but found only that relentless stare. "It made me hide inside myself," I told her, more softly. Then, with lips that could barely move around the words, "it made me quit trying."

"And now that it's gone?" she asked.

"I don't know any other way to be," I told her in a voice even I recognized as a whine.

This time the eyes came straight for mine. "How old are you?" she asked.

"Thirty-six," I told her. "How old are you?"

"Twenty-one. It's too soon to quit trying," she told me.

I looked down at the pie. "I suppose so," I told her. "But…" But what? How could I explain to a young girl about the demons of the past, how they seize your reins and drive you. How I hadn't the courage to wrest control. How it was ever so much easier to fade into incompleteness.

"But you have been formed by deformity," she said. I looked up, searching those haunted eyes. "That is the silent half of any language," she said. "The words behind the spoken words. The words that twist meaning, until meaning itself is deformed."

I stared at her, suddenly afraid. "What are you talking about?" I asked.

"There are monsters inside us all, Mr. Deeters," she said. "They see us, and they are enraged." I knew, I was sure that she was speaking of my brother. That she knew something about my brother.

"Why?" I asked, afraid of the answer.

"Because they cannot take full control; they can only twist us. They are the silent half, moving. They are the Other."

Chapter 3

April 1990 – September 1990

GILEAD

One day I saw what was making Mr. Deeters decay. He carries a ghost beside him, a little boy. The ghost is chained to him in some way that Mr. Deeters controls. The ghost is eating away at him. But there's something else that's desperate to grow, to take the ghost's place. I don't know which will win.

Mr. Deeters likes to read. I meet him at the library, then we drink tea in a restaurant that is always the same. Mr. Deeters puts aside the ghost as we drink. Then it is easier to look at him. He is tall and thin, with beautiful eyes. When he walks, it looks as if he thinks the earth will open up and swallow him. Everything about him is careful. He spends his days sticking small, neat pins into details, securing them. He presents himself as neatly folded, trim, contained. But after awhile, I started to see what a mask this all was. The real man—that potato in the basement—was still inside, growing desperate for the light. I was so curious. I came back each week, just to see what happened.

MR. DEETERS

Gilead's line about the monsters within was the first hint I had that the source of her terror was from the inside. Up until the time of this conversation, I'd assumed that Gilead's monsters were all in the family—her mother and sister, long on make-up and short on taste.

A couple of months after our library routine got started, both Gilead and the exterior monsters started showing up at my church—

a source of immediate embarrassment to me and considerable conversational interest to the rest of the congregation. It was summer, and her mother's pink coat had been traded in for a kind of tent with large, obscene, and excruciatingly ugly flowers. The sister had donned a pale green polyester pant suit which highlighted each bulge, while picking up the strains of artificial coloring in her badly shorn hair. Gilead wore a white cotton dress, making her look like a perfect candidate for Sacrificial Virgin.

I was stunned by the way the family assumed a relationship with me. They cornered me in a pew right after the service. "We've heard so many excellent things about this preacher," said the sister (referring, I assumed, to our priest). "And I must say that all of them are true. Don't you agree, Mama?" The tent bobbled enthusiastically beside her as I looked for a way to make my escape. Gilead was gazing at the chapel windows with a new look. I allowed myself a peek at her, while straining over her sister's head toward someone, anyone, I could justify speaking with. Gilead looked serene. The look stopped me.

I turned toward the window that held her attention, seeing for the umpteenth time the angel Gabriel standing a lily away from the Virgin Mary. "Do you like our windows?" I asked her.

"Oh, Gilly loves windows!" the mother answered. "She just spends hours by them each day."

Gilead turned toward me and spoke. "I like angels," she said.

I considered this. "There's a picture of two angels in the Sunday School room downstairs," I told her. "Would you like to see them?"

Gilead looked startled, but her sister said, "Go ahead, Gilly, don't be shy. We'll wait for you outside." (God must have answered my prayer—we were to be separated from that family!)

"Did you enjoy the sermon?" I asked as we reached the bottom of the stairs.

Gilly looked at me blankly. "Didn't listen," she said. My face must have fallen a bit; why was she here then? As if reading my mind, she said, "Mother's in one of her religious periods, so we thought we'd try here."

"Ah," I said, my heart thunking. "Does that mean we'll have the pleasure of your mother's company from here on out?"

Gilead smiled. Oh dear, I hadn't meant it to sound that sarcastic. "These things generally don't last for more than a month," she said.

"A month," I repeated, thinking that would certainly be long enough to risk my reputation. "And then does the whole family stop coming?"

"Usually," she said. "Though sometimes I come on my own. Actually, I spend a lot of time in churches. It's nice to get away."

"I'm sure," I said, a little too earnestly.

Having the Grasons at my church meant I had to make adjustments, and rather quickly. For one thing, I'd been dating the third grade Sunday School teacher for the past two years, a relationship I'd been meaning to shut off (too many people, including the teacher, were starting to mention marriage) but had been too lazy to leave (she made love and muffins with the same fluffy sweetness). The teacher was fortunately away visiting her sister in Norfolk the morning the Grasons first showed, but I knew that at least a dozen people would tell her as soon as she returned. I decided to tell Hilma (the teacher) that she was just too good for me. Alternatively, I could tell her I knew the person she'd visited in Norfolk wasn't her sister but a man, and just didn't feel I could trust her anymore. Or I could spread that rumor. None of these ploys looked like they'd have the immediate effect I needed; all of them would probably bring about dozens of letters and calls and female go-betweens and little chats with the church deacons (women can make things dreadfully uncomfortable for bachelors in a small town, which is one of the reasons why I generally date women from Easton instead). I decided to stick with telling her she was too good for me. It had all the power of truth: she was.

Next, I needed to find a way to integrate Gilead into the church body without unnecessarily offending Hilma. One way to lure Gilead that occurred to me immediately was the church's book discussion group—a meeting started over 20 years ago by women wanting to read the larger books of the Bible, but which had fortunately degenerated into a far more secular singles club. Gilly seemed to like books. And it was a place where we'd never run into Hilma.

I expected some resistance on Gilly's part; she seems terribly shy. But Gilly agreed to go (with Missy practically pushing her out the door), and then took to the group immediately, giving her complete attention to each speaker—including the bores, who were starved for such stuff. She spoke so rarely (in that faint voice of hers), approaching the works in such an angular way, that the group treated each spare analysis as oddly sacred.

Thankfully, her mother and sister tired of the Episcopal faith almost immediately, appearing again only for two weeks. Also thankfully, Gilly continued to appear. I took this as a sign of her deepening friendship for me, joined her in the back pews, and graduallly moved her forward to the seat in which I felt most comfortable—always being careful to leave the church before Hilma came upstairs.

Then, one Sunday during prayer, she reached over and took my hand. I was entirely consumed by the warmth of that fragile pressure. Lacing her fingers into mine, I held her for the duration of the service. Dear God, I thought between the Amens, don't let her let go.

Driving her home that day, I parked beside the woods near her neighborhood and suggested we go for a walk. Obediently, she left the car and steered her feet along the dirt path between the fragrant evergreens. I took hold of her hand and pointed out pine cones and birds as we passed—anything to keep her mind focused on the here and now. Then, safely out of sight of the road, I turned her toward me and bent down to kiss her. She looked up with those haunted eyes, but did not shrink. I pressed my lips on hers as gently as I could, and moved my arms around her, feeling her shiver. Still, she did not pull back. I felt a rising ache in my loins of amazing intensity, and kept her body away. I was afraid of what might happen if she touched me there. Moving my lips from hers, I kissed her face, her eyes, her hair. She lowered her head shyly, but allowed me to kiss her. I wanted her; I was frightening her. She moved her head up; put her lips tentatively on mine. I kissed her hard, sucking up the warmth of her mouth. She moaned and shivered, pulling her sweet body close to mine. I felt my hands against her back, pressing her into me, felt the sharpness of my need of her. Sweat began to pour from my forehead; I wanted to throw her down and take her on the forest floor; I wanted to possess her, to crush her, to rip her apart and pour myself into her.

She pushed herself away from me with tiny, steel arms; I opened my eyes and saw the wild terror in hers. I went limp. I kissed her slowly again, a soothing series of kisses around her face. "Come home with me," I said, kissing the sides of her ear.

She pulled away from me slightly with a puzzled look. Her lips formed, but did not pronounce, the word: Home? I nodded. She looked at me, completely baffled. "But how," she finally asked, "how can I leave my family?"

Ah, the monsters, I thought. Still holding the reins. "You must leave your family," I told her. "Whether you come with me or not, you must leave your family. It's the only chance you have of surviving."

More staring, followed by a careful study of the ground around us. "I don't know if I can," she finally said.

"I'll help you," I said quickly. It occurred to me later that I didn't know if she meant, I don't know if I can leave, or I don't know if I can survive.

Both parts are in question.

MISSY

The next natural step was to take Gilead to Mr. Deeters' church, a place we fortunately didn't have to revisit often before the girl was going on her own (the people there have dreadful taste in clothes). Gilly likes churches; they're quiet. When she was a little girl and ran away from time to time, as little girls do, we'd always find her hiding in a church, reading the missals or memorizing the scriptural quotes. In fact, there was a period —even more irritating than this mute period—when she only spoke in scriptural selections. Which drove us all batty, of course.

The time finally came when Gilead and Mr. Deeters were stepping out, first to the book discussion group at the church and later to our local theater. Mr. Deeters coming to pick her up required some vigorous cleaning of the living room on our part (and I have to say, in all fairness to our aunt, that she was wonderfully cooperative), as well as snaring Freddy's help in keeping mother away (not so easily achieved—Freddy doesn't work by faints).

The cleaning and clearing were nothing compared with the night Mr. Deeters was invited to dinner. Mother was unfortunately practicing her radish-and-garlic diet at the time, which the whole family was anxious for her to change. She suggested returning to either the grapefruit diet or the high protein one, but the former has such dire effects on her stomach and the latter on her breath, we were hard bent to dissuade her. Aunt finally got her started on the Pritikin diet, a short-lived but glorious choice—Mr. Deeters is a vegetarian.

At that dinner, I learned that Mr. Deeters' interest in Gilead had gone far beyond receiving her head-bobbing assents and haunted-eye looks. Mr. Deeters is quite interested in the phenomena of twins, particularly identical twins. Mother has this belief that Gilly and I are twins, sharing the same set of chromosomes (although, as a fictional character, I have nothing in common with any member of my family except an alphabet).

Mr. Deeters believes that twins share a special gift of ESP, a subject mother knows oodles about, which blessedly took us off the subject of diets. He then asked if we'd ever been tested for ESP. Well, no, we hadn't (I don't write those sorts of books). Mr. Deeters had a pack of special cards in his suit jacket, and invited Gilead and me to sit down on opposite sides of our dazzlingly clean living room for the test.

Well, you can imagine how I felt. ESP is one of those things mere humans cling to in their longing to become fictional; fictional characters like myself are already constructed of imagination, and have no need for such artifice. Of course there was no possibility of ESP between Gilly and a person of my character. Still, I could see that my plan for attaching Mr. Deeters to the family hinged on this craving of his, and having spent a lifetime learning to read my sister (whose words are both spare and false) it was no trouble giving him what he wanted. We did so well, in fact, that Mr. Deeters insisted on repeating the test several times to check the results.

"Why, Mr. Deeters," I said, "if you want to know us this well, we'll just have to make you a member of the family."

"Oh, Michelle!" mother said (that awful name again), "is that what the Great Beyond would want?"

To Mr. Deeters' puzzled stare, Freddy said, "That's a faint friend of Missy's."

"You have to expect a few oddities in a household of twins," I told him. "In fact, there are many things about twins I'm sure you'd never guess."

"Like what?" he asked, his eyes squeezing into a stare.

He had me stumped there. "You'll find out from Gilead," I suggested, knowing that this mystery would simply be swallowed up by the mystery that was my sister. "Why don't you take Mr. Deeters out to the porch, honey, so you two can talk about it?"

"That should be enlightening," Freddy added. The jerk. Perhaps I'll write him out of my novel, too.

What happened between them on the porch was apparently enough to whet Mr. Deeters' appetite for a graphic understanding of twins. Two weeks later, he asked my mother for Gilead's hand in marriage. One month after that, on September 23, 1990, they were wed.

And now, our grocery bills paid for life, I can go and write the next chapter.

MR. DEETERS

The dinner with Gilead's family was theater of the grotesque—an exercise of will in which I forced myself to overcome both a recurrent gag response and my natural aversion to chatting up bizarre people. I did obtain some astonishing results on the ESP tests, though. Gilead, as I suspected, is amazingly intuitive; how else can I explain her understanding of my brother?

It became obvious that this girl is too frightened, and the family too smothering, for us to have an affair. In fact, I became convinced that the only path I could take to extract the girl from her family was down the aisle of a church. So I buried the arguments I've used all my life to maintain my single state, and married her. Now she's mine. And I am hers.

Chapter 4

September 24, 1990

FREDDY

The bride wore yellow. Isn't that how all wedding stories start? The bride wore yellow, saturated with zillions of tiny dohickeys called seed pearls. The seed pearls were the other twin's idea—the kind of crazy-making project Missy loves. Missy is the kind of woman—girl, really; the twins are only 21—who paints the living room baseboards each month just to keep them from looking too dusty.

So Missy spent a month inflicting pearls on yellow imitation damask, while Gilly wallowed in bride-like dreams by the window. Actually, I don't know what Gilly was wallowing in. Gilly had spent the better part of three years by one window or another, reading every kind of book there is or glazing her eyes toward the outdoors and running a finger delicately around her throat. She almost never talks at home. Oh, she'll say a word now and then under pressure, extreme pressure—a fact that added drama to the wedding march. While the guests were murmuring over the color choice of her wedding gown, our family was gripping the pews, wondering if Gilly would be able to say her line. It's a funny thing but, if you don't talk for awhile, your throat kind of gets out of practice.

Anyway, the bride wore yellow because yellow is Gilly's lucky color. I know this because, on mornings when mother comes out of her conference with whatever power she's believing in at the moment and announces that Today is Not a Lucky Day, Gilly wanders off, drifting in later bedecked in yellow. It matches her skin. She looked hideous, though not because she's an ugly girl. Actually, Gilly can be drop-dead gorgeous, if you like anorexia. But she'd insisted on yellow, Missy told us while she studded away. You wouldn't think Gilly capable of insisting on anything—some days I think if I told her to go lie in her coffin, she'd agree—but she does get into moods sometimes, and then there's no stopping her.

And was she ever in a mood this month! Gilly usually creeps around so stealthily that whole days can go by and I won't remember seeing her. It's gotten to be something of a family joke. I remember starting up from my seat at dinner one night, saying "Has anyone seen Gilly lately?" Only to find that she was sitting right next to me at the table.

But this month, her slinking around became downright noisy. She pouted. She set her mouth, and wouldn't answer any questions about the wedding, but shook her head No to most suggestions. Missy finally stopped asking, and the other two women took their cue from her.

My job in the family (just about my only job—I've been relieved of most responsibilities, not being able to hold any) is to ask the obvious questions. So I asked. "Do you want to marry this man?" I said—in the kitchen, where she'd gone to make tea. She's nuts about tea; I knew I had her attention at least until the water boiled.

Gilly looked down, studying what has to be one of the more boring examples of linoleum.

I knew what she was thinking (or at least I thought I did. Living with the mute gives you a false sense of being able to read their mind). So I said, "Are you doing this just because Missy wants you to?" That got a definite glance in my direction. "Do you like him?" I asked, softer now. A shy smile; more linoleum-gazing. "Are you afraid?" That was a safe guess; Gilly's always afraid. But she knit her brows together, a straining look that often precedes a word. I waited. Sometimes the words don't come; they never come if you rush them.

Finally she said, as the water began to boil, "What will become of the family?"

"Us?" I asked, in mock shock. "Why, we're Grasons, child. We're just the happiest-go-luckiest family in Cambridge. We'll do great." She shot me her You're-full-of-shit look, so I told her the obvious (the other job I have). "Missy wants this, so she must think it's good for the family."

Gilly heaved a sigh. I knew what she was thinking. What's Missy up to?

◇ ◇ ◇

It was a funky wedding in its own way. For one thing, there was the choice of bride and groom. Gilly has the drawing power of a fresh box of kitty litter for a cat as far as men are concerned, and I always figured Missy would train some likely man to keep going there eventually. But Nate Deeters! Jesus, what a choice. The man is thin-lipped, thin-haired, tight-fisted, tidy, and I think totally insane. For a storekeeper. He's really into ESP, for one thing. And twins, for another. Just what kind of weirdness is he getting out of this marriage?

Nate owns Zippy Trip, a fairly inconvenient convenience/grocery store that's the last thing out of town. It caters to the things you're always out of—milk, batteries, small expensive packages of produce, Kleenex. What it needs is a large, square, gossipy woman (like my mother) who's good with figures (unlike my mother) to serve as bartender to the milk-deprived. What it's got is Nate Deeters, watching the fishbowl mirrors for signs of snitching and raising the cost of living for the good citizens of Cambridge.

And Gilly. Now it can have Gilly.

How did that happen? Was Deeters completely set up? He can't have any clear idea of what kind of insanity he's just married into. But he's not blind (just nearsighted). And despite the fact that Missy pushed him with a cattleprod into this marriage, I think...I believe that he truly wants Gilly.

But why?

GILEAD

My wedding night. "I changed the sheets," he tells me. Laundry smells mixed with aftershave. Lights off. He locks the door. I face the window. The curtains are closed. Moonlight leaking through the pattern. Long arms beneath pajama top. No pajama bottom. Careful unbuttoning of my nightgown. Soft lips against my mouth.

A face, I see a face. The night-man's face. Eyes that slick over me, leaving me greasy. Sweat, like small tears, forming along his brow.

I go blank.

Then it is morning. My husband, in white jockey shorts, sits at the edge of the bed. The elastic lynches his waist; small slabs of him ooze over the side. I touch the slabs, curious at their firmness. He giggles, turns to look at me. Apology rings his eyes with small o's. "Poor little thing," he says. "I guess you wanted to marry someone younger."

I am married to Mr. Deeters. Husband. I must call him Husband now. My fingers stray to his back, the V of sparse fur nestling between his shoulder blades. My fingers reach something peculiar, stop. I rise to look. The sheets, their laundry smell gone, replaced, drop away. I am naked. I pull back, ashamed. He looks at me with gentle sorrow. "Don't be shy, Gilead," he says, cupping my chin. "We're married now. It's all right."

I swaddle in bedclothes, eyes returning to the V-shaped animal on my husband's back. He holds himself rigid, clutching one brown slipper. I kneel on the bed behind his back. My fingers reach toward the fur, feeling down its middle. A zipper-shaped scar is outlined beneath my fingertips. I trace it, over and over. It feels electric, warm. I nuzzle my ear into the fur, straining to listen to it. My arms go around my husband's body as I lay my head against his back. Holding his protruding stomach, I am clutched close to the scar. His long, thin hand rests on mine. Tentative. I feel his hesitancy. It makes me safe. I am so comfortable.

"You've found the spot," he says. His voice is soft. "I kinda thought you would. That's where the growth was." He seems happy.

I nod, decide to speak. "It speaks to me," I say.

He goes stiff, straining. "What does he say?" he asks. His voice is urgent. I don't know the answer.

I shake my head. "It hums," I explain.

He is clutching at my hand, pulling me closer to the scar. "I need to know what he says, Gilly. Only you can tell me what he says." I don't know what he means. He's become so strange. I pull away, turn over in the bed, clutch my knees. I feel his intense stare; close my eyes against it. "Is it that bad?" he asks.

I don't understand. "It only hums," I say again.

He sighs, long and loud. Then, "Would you like a cup of tea?"

I nod. He leaves.

The morning pools peacefully, with the two of us in bathrobes reading the paper. Husband dislikes breakfast; I am relieved. I dislike eating. I must make lunch; sandwiches. I make sandwich spread. I find mineral water in the refrigerator; decide to pour it for our lunch. I reach for a glass. It falls; breaks. It is shattered. Husband shouts from the living room, "What happened?" I tell him it's okay. I stare at the broken glass for a long time; go woozy. Go blank. Then I awake. I am sitting on the floor with a shard of broken glass in my hand. My wrist is bleeding. I stop the blood with a napkin. Where is the rest of the glass? I stand; run cold water over my wrist. I look at the bowl of sandwich spread. The glass shards are there, poked in. I throw the spread out; start again.

I hand him the plate with my unbandaged hand. I am shaking. He kisses my fingers. It is very romantic. It is egg salad. He eats it, little bits of mayonaisse drooling onto his fingers. He wipes frequently. I chew mine; swallowing is painful.

The phone rings. "Who is it?" he asks me. It rings again. I never answer phones. "Do you know who it is, Gilead?" he asks, as it rings a third time. "Take a guess."

"Missy," I answer. Who else would bother a honeymoon couple on their first day?

"Deeters," he answers. "Yes, she's right here." He's beaming as he hands me the phone.

I nod into the phone, forgetting she can't see me. Missy's voice thuds in my ear. I nod some more. I reach for a pencil, turn over a used envelope. I take notes; hang up. The envelope is transferred to my husband's hand.

"What's this?" he asks, staring at the list—mayonnaise, a roasting chicken, a can of creamed corn—"groceries?"—two ripe tomatoes, a head of lettuce, Duncan Hines spice cake—"we're closed today"—cream cheese, a box of 10XX sugar—"do they expect you to deliver this today?"

My husband is shouting. He expects an answer. He doesn't want to hear yes. "Monday," I tell him.

MR. DEETERS

If in-laws are the permanent wedding present, the Grasons are the ultimate white elephant. The spacey mother, the bossy twin sister, the worthless brother. Not one of them has lifted a finger to add to the family income since they arrived in that grotesque VW bus. The mother gets a small pension from her dead husband's employer (I believe he sold shoelaces—not a sign of ambition or enterprise), but for some reason no one ever talks about why there's no insurance. "Oh, yes, we had a policy," Missy assured me one day, "but of course, given the circumstances...." she trailed off, dribbling thought along with her. It does no good to ask for specifics. The family looks at you as if you're some kind of unfortunate nit to be flicked away when you ask questions—or just ignored.

Or used. My questions go unnoticed in this family; my resources do not. The first day—the first day!—of our honeymoon, mind you, they called and asked for groceries. Gilly tried to pretend they didn't want them until Monday, in that way she has of trying to soothe me, dear thing. But by mid-afternoon, Freddy showed up at the door expecting goodies. I gave him a firm piece of my mind—probably the firmest piece of any man's mind he's had in a long while. The boy is simply drowning in females over there.

"And furthermore," I told him, "if you think my marriage to your sister will bring you unlimited free groceries, you've got another think coming." Well of course that's exactly what he was thinking, or at least what his sister was thinking. Michelle, the one with the randomly changing name. She's behind all this. She must think I'm a complete idiot not to notice.

So Freddy slinked off, the eternal message-bearer. Pretty soon the phone rang. "I'll take it," I told Gilly, whose shoulders rounded with each ring. It was Missy. I told her Gilly was busy, and prepared to confront her with the cabal over my groceries.

"Well, my goodness, of course she is, you old devil," Missy said. "You must think me perfectly dreadful bothering you two lovebirds like this on today of all days." I was about to agree, but her nattering was relentless and without interstices. "Of course I know what you're up to and think it's perfectly fine, I'm sure you're a real gentleman and of course poor dear Gilly must think so too. After all, she's your wife now, isn't she?"

"I'll have you know…" I began. I must confess I was spluttering by this time, and not sure which hideous innuendo I was about to dispel with what truth. She shut me off before I had time to accurately formulate exactly how I felt about her wicked and oblique accusations. I'd gotten as far as "my wife and I would like to be left in…"

"Of course you would," Missy said, two or three times, jerking me out of a conversational path that was going straight towards polarity, "and we have every intention of leaving you be. The Grasons do not interfere," she announced in that righteous tone of voice people use to tell bald-faced lies. "It's just that," here her voice became tremulous and drippy, "you have the rest of your lives for that…sort of thing. But here, today," she said, sucking in her breath, "well—no, I'm afraid to tell you."

I doubted that. "What?" I asked.

"You'll think us very poor managers, I'm afraid," she said. I did. "But, well, what with the demands of the wedding yesterday—it was lovely, of course, but so wearing on us all, especially dear mother—I'm afraid we forgot, we were unable—oh, I'll just say it. We didn't get by the bank. And now," here she sobbed, "we're alone up here with no," she whispered this, "nothing to eat."

"Oh, for Pete's sakes—no one runs completely out of groceries," I said. Loud, sloppy sobs greeted this statement. "How about the canapes?" I asked. Missy and her aunt had spent hours squirting cheese-squeeze onto white crackers and slicing stuffed olives over the top.

"Why, they're all gone. Oh I do hope our guests enjoyed them. They were such trouble to make. Do you know we used eight boxes of crackers? Eight whole boxes. And...."

"There were no leftovers? I thought I saw quite a few on the table." Specifics, that's what this family is lacking.

"Oh, my, no. Of course there was the odd occasional one here and there, but we, well, you know. Anyway. So I don't mean to interrupt you, not for a second, but I thought perhaps, you're such a kind and understanding man, just the sort to make my sister happy, she does adore you so—she tells me that all the time—and I thought..."

Adoring Gilly was standing by the window, her pain at this conversation transparent. Watching her, I felt stirrings from the night before, her unexpected openness, her need, the sweetness of her warmth as she received my body. "Send Freddy," I told Missy. "Just this once. After this, no more. Do I make myself clear?"

"Oh, Mr. Deeters, what a wonderful man you are! I was just saying to mother..."

"I'll leave the key to the store in the mailbox, and I want it returned. We do not wish to be disturbed."

"No, indeedy. I understand," she said, practically winking into the phone.

I hung up sharply. I took the key from my leather key chain, and attached it with a clip to the inside of the mailbox. Then I walked to the bedroom and closed the curtains. I walked back to my wife, shuddering by the living room window. "Gilly," I whispered. She looked up with frightened eyes. "It's all right now; they'll leave us alone." She shook her head. I touched her cheek, her hair, the lids of those rounded eyes. "Come," I said. Her opened eyes showed question marks. "I want you," I told her. Something slid across her eyes—a door. She came to me, and opened.

GILEAD

There was a knock on the door. It was Freddy, wanting his groceries. Husband answered it, said sharp words. Freddy peered around him, waving at me. I waved back. I was happy to see him. He left. Husband returned, picked up the book he was reading. I turned back to the window, watched Freddy receeding.

There is a phone call. Missy. Husband's face turns red. He splutters harsh words into the telephone. I rise to move, but can't. I am paralyzed, standing next to the window. Sometimes if I stare out the window, the whole day will fold around me, stretch through my fingertips and disappear. Husband stops me, folds me to him. His lips press hard on mine. "I want you," he says. "My beautiful wife." I must not refuse. Everything goes black.

The blackness always ends. Each morning when I awaken, we are lying in bed, naked. I snuggle up against him, grasping the hair on his chest. It is so comforting. He strokes my hair. "You're a very sexy woman," he tells me. His voice sounds different. It's lower, more raspy.

"Are you happy?" I ask without thinking. It's something I've said before, after the blackness.

"Very," he says, still stroking my hair.

Weeks go by. He still smiles at me in the morning. I think I will be all right.

One morning my arm wraps around him as I cuddle side to side against his warm body. My fingers reach the animal shape on his back, trace its electrical warmth. I close my eyes to see it better. My firm, well-bound husband suddenly becomes porous in this spot. It is a fragile state, one he cannot maintain for long. I am so touched by this, his willingness to open to me.

"Gilly," he whispers, "what do you see?"

It hurts him to ask this; his voice scrapes at his throat. I turn him over, put my ear to the scar. "Confusion," I tell him as the sound spurts out at me in tangled shrieks. I close my eyes again, trying to untangle the sounds. There are too many. I stop trying. I rest, breathe, letting the shapes of the sounds dart and weave through my mind. Then I tell him.

"There used to be something here, something real. Then it was empty, hollow." He nods.

"Now it is filling up again. You are filling it up again." He nods again. I listen, trying to understand the shrieks, the reason for the shrieks.

Oh. Oh, I see. I sit up, push him onto his back. I feel like screaming at him; I want to hit him, hit him with words. But he looks at me with child eyes. Children are too vulnerable. It would be evil to hit him.

I speak as softly as I can, stroke his face as I push words at him. But I can't think how to say it. It is Jeremiah, a quote. My people have committed two sins, it says. They have forsaken me, the fountain of living waters, and hewn themselves cisterns, broken cisterns, that can hold no water. That's what I see. How can I explain it?

"You have left something precious," I tell him. He nods. "But you are building something false. Husband," I tell him, stroking his face, "husband—you must not do this. You must keep looking. You must find the light."

Chapter 5

October 1990

FREDDY

Life at home has been weird since the wedding. You wouldn't think the absence of someone who never said anything, never did anything, barely ate anything and rarely made a ripple in the day would make that much difference. But it's a little like the old story of the family with the elephant in the living room that no one admitted was there. We've all been so careful to walk around Gilly. Now that she's gone, our tiptoeing around seems bizarre.

Not that I ever say this to Gilly. Or anything else, for that matter—I've grown out of the habit of saying anything to Gilly. Instead, I usually find myself wandering down to her house a couple of times a week, sometimes on a mission from Missy to get groceries (if I absolutely can't find any excuse not to), and sometimes because I just happen to find myself in the area. Then we have one of these real quiet visits. I'll plop down and watch her T.V. for awhile, or make myself a snack and eat it at her table. It sounds kinda awkward, but it's not. Gilly's about the most comfortable person I've ever found to be with. She smiles at my jokes and listens to my stories and folds my silences into her own. Still, I wish I knew what she was thinking.

There was a time when Gilly and I could talk, because Gilly could talk. Though I remember her more for what she did than for what she said. Like the times when our father, Rod the Avenger, lit into me over something or other (there was always something. Or another), probably egged on by Missy's details and mother's hand-clutching Oh-I-don't-know-what-we're-going-to-do-with-that-boy whines. "Well, I do!" Pa would always say, taking off his belt or grabbing the fire tongs or whatever weapon came to hand (weapons always came to Pa's hand, like magic). Then he'd beat the crap out of me, and I'd wind up in my room, licking my wounds and listening to Missy rehash all my wrongs downstairs as mother whimpered. There's no other word for it. Dilly-Dally Sally, we used to call mother—queen of the whiners.

But Gilly would sneak up with milk and peanut butter sandwiches—or beer and chips and a rope, in our teenaged years—and give me a smile. That's all. That was enough.

Gilly gave comfort; she never rescued. Missy was the rescuer. Missy had all these schemes for making Pa buy things, or do things, or accept things, usually involving lots of food and Gilly as the sacrificial lamb. Missy would fix Pa's favorite dinner, plump his chair pillow, and send Gilly for his slippers. Then, while Gilly was getting them, Missy would whisper to Pa that Gilly really needs such and such, or Gilly didn't want to tell you, but this really terrible thing happened, please don't be too hard on her.

Pa would turn and watch Gilly coming down the stairs, watch her bend and bow over his size 12 feet and start to put his slippers on. Then he'd reach out with those huge hands like slabs of clawed meat, pull her hair until her eyes stared at his, and glare at her until she started to shake. He'd grin at her, turn to the rest of the family as we bunched around, nervously waiting for a verdict—and agree to anything Missy had asked for.

Gilly never asked for anything. Gilly never rescued. She never rescued, and neither did I. I swept up. Freddy the sweeper.

There were nights—Christ, it's hard to write about these things. There were the nights of the screams. I'd hear them, coming from Gilly's bedroom, and go stiff, like I was paralyzed or something. I never went in at night. I used to ask about them in the beginning. Mother or Missy would tell me Gilly had nightmares, and not to bother her about it. Sometimes if she didn't come down for breakfast, I'd go up and find her tied to the bed or locked in the closet.

Curled up. Stiff. The first time, I ran downstairs to tell mother. She just hummed at me, um hum, that's nice, dear. So I grabbed Missy and pulled her upstairs to the closet. "Daddy's just playing a little game," Missy said, pulling Gilly out of the closet as if she'd done it a thousand times before. "Come on, Gilly, for heaven's sake, hurry up, you'll make us late for school again. Get her clothes, Freddy."

I know it sounds inhuman. Thinking back on it now, it seems insane that I never told anyone, never did anything, never called the cops or the child welfare types or even told a neighbor or a teacher. I don't know why I didn't. I guess it's because I was a kid, maybe, or because everybody else just treated it as normal.

I read a bunch of books once about the Holocaust—on the sly, of course. I had to protect my reputation as a juvenile delinquent; nobody but Gilly ever knew how much I read. Anyway, they were trying to explain why the Jews in those camps almost never fought back. I didn't have any trouble understanding it—that's just what happens when madmen are in control. Like in our house—I never let myself think about what was happening in our family; I just accepted it. My job was to sweep up afterwards, to pull Gilly out, to untie her, to rub her wrists and find her clothes and thank whatever gods were left in the world that it wasn't me. Later when she started slashing at her wrists, I was the one who bandaged and squirted antiseptic and took away the razor blades. No, I never told anyone. Who was there to tell? I swept up; Freddy the sweeper. That's what I did the day our father died. Or at least that's what I thought I was doing that day. I know it sounds crazy. But it's how I survived; it's how we all survived.

◊ ◊ ◊

Even when Gilly did talk, you never knew who you were talking to. I remember the first day I met Rita. That's one of the names she calls herself (we got a lot of names in this family). I was working on a go-cart one morning—I must have been 7 or 8, I guess—when Gilly wanders out with her dolls. She was big on dolls. We had this huge old evergreen in the front yard where we used to play. It was a great place; we made it into forts a lot of times, or Missy would set up one of her big, fancy houses or clubs and decide who could come in and what they could do. It was pretty early in the morning, though, and Missy must have been asleep, because here comes Gilly in her old shorts with her dolls, all alone.

I liked to get up early and work on my stuff. Tempers in our house worked like steam engines; they took awhile to heat up. So the morning hours, especially on the weekends, nobody was up or mad enough to do anything. I guess Gilly liked it too; she used to charge out of there with the sunrise.

Most little girls like to dress up their dolls; Gilly undressed them. I think this was the first time I noticed that. I got us some powdered doughnuts from the kitchen, and slipped under the boughs of the tree. There was Gilly with her legs spread, the dolls piled between her limbs. One of the dolls was in her lap with its dress wrenched up. No underpants. Gilly had her fingers on the doll's crotch. She sat there, cooing.

"Hey, Gilly, want a doughnut?" I asked, taking one for myself and passing her the box.

"Don't call me that—it ain't my name," she said. I figured we were playing pretend. Gilly is great at pretend.

I dropped the box by her side, and sat down. "Oh, yeah?" I asked. "What's your name then?"

"Rita," she said, diving into the doughnuts. Gilly's usually a picky eater, but that morning she acted like she was starving or something. She stuffed a whole doughnut into her mouth, and picked up another.

"Better not eat 'em all, or Missy will give us heck," I said. Then I added, "Rita." I watched her down her second doughnut. She looked at me and grinned, powdered sugar all over her mouth. "So, whatcha doing?" I asked.

"Playing with Gilly," she said, stroking the doll with her fingernail. Something about the way she said it made me feel like barfing. I went back to my go-cart.

◊ ◊ ◊

Then there was Smart Lady. Smart Lady started as a game between us, the first time we seriously talked about Pa. This was on a day after one of his binges, when we'd all been beaten—even Missy. Gilly and I were up early, and decided without talking to take a walk. It was a nutty thing to do, must have been 15 degrees outside and of course we couldn't find anything like gloves or hats (we didn't have the kind of house where you could expect to find matching shoes, let alone gloves). So we watched our breath do dragon imitations and pounded down the highway near our home. "I'm gonna kill him," I said for what must have been the millionth time in my life.

"What if we did?" Gilly said.

"Huh?"

"What if we really did?"

"What do you mean, really?" I asked.

"Let's pretend," she said, her standard beginning to group fantasizing. That sounded safer, so I agreed. "I'll be Smart Lady," she said, "and you'll be—who d'ya wanna be, Freddy?"

"John Wayne. And I'll be about 100 feet tall and have big muscles and...."

"No, dummy, I mean what name? You're gonna be a kid."

"I can't be a kid. Kids could never kill him."

"Smart Lady can," she said. Dead serious. "Smart Lady's smart," she added.

"Okay, I'll be Stan. Stan the Man."

"Stan the boy. This is real, Freddy. You gotta pretend right, or I won't play."

"Okay, just Stan, then. How're we gonna do it? Smart Lady," I said.

"We could shoot him," she said.

"Oh, that's smart. Where're we gonna get a gun? And where do we put the body? And what if somebody hears us?"

Smart Lady thought for awhile as I walked along beside her, rubbing my red hands. "You could dig a grave in the woods," she said. "And we could tell him there was something we wanted him to see in the woods, and take him down, and show him the grave, and then shoot him, and he'd fall into it, and nobody'd ever know. And we could get Pa's rifle, and sneak it back into the house."

Pa kept the gun for deer hunting, locked away in the basement. I didn't think we'd ever sneak the gun away from him, and said so.

"Sure we can," said Smart Lady. "I'm smart. I'll find a way."

But she didn't, of course—though we talked about it for years. As we got older, we stopped talking about killing Pa. But I'd still see Smart Lady occasionally. She'd sit in my room, swinging her leg back and forth and talking in this high, squeaky voice. She knew stuff about my girlfriends and could figure out what made them act so strange. She could figure out stuff about her boyfriends, too. But she'd never do anything about it. I'd tell her she had to make them stop doing that stuff, or tell them she wouldn't go out with them. But she'd just say how sad they were or how upset they were about their parents and how they had to take it out on someone.

It really made me mad. So I'd play my ultimate card: "What if Pa finds out you're dating, huh? What then?"

"He won't," she say in this dead-serious voice. "I'm too smart. You know that, Freddy."

"Oh, yeah?" I said, angry now. "What if I tell him?"

She looked me straight in the eye. "You won't," she said, quietly.

I dropped it. I knew she was right.

I suppose I could have asked Smart Lady about this husband of hers. But I haven't seen Smart Lady in a long time. Not since that last night with Pa when she seemed to disappear, replaced by something much more frightening. I saw that night that Gilly could defend herself, though it scared the shit out of me to see how she did it. It also scared the shit out of me to see how I reacted.

By the next day, Gilly had gone limp, then freezing into some other person. Sometimes I don't even know who's there anymore in Gilly. We never talk about it. We've never even talked about the night Pa died. I'm not even sure she remembers it.

What I want to know is this—which of these people married Deeters? And just what does her husband think he's getting for a wife?

Chapter 6

December 1990

SALLY

Diet Diary

8:30   One cup coffee, with small dollop cream (half and half) and teeny teaspoon sugar. Plus a smidge of danish, no more than half. Lemon.

   Feeling: Sleepy, but excited to be in touch with the spirits of the day. Good horoscope. Money in the offing?

10:00   One onion bagel with just a smear of cream cheese, and a few sips of coke, 5-6 oz.

   Feeling: Stressed. Sister so nasty about the money. She doesn't believe I'll win the lottery.

11:20 One small sausage pizza with lots of green pepper, full of vitamin C. One cream soda. One brownie, nuts knocked off.

   Feeling: Hopeful. Lottery ticket has numbers 3 and 7 in it. Numbers add up to 21. Sure to win!

12:30 Lunch—leftover casserole. Michelle is such a fine cook. Sprinkled just a little extra cheese over the top. One small salad, with low-calorie dressing (bleu cheese).

   Feeling: Mild irritation. Missy believes I should visit Mr. and Mrs. Deeters today. I have already been to town. Really, she is quite impossible.

2:30 Yuk-Yuk bar and Taco chips at Mr. Deeters' store, finished on the way home.

Feeling: In tears. Mr. Deeters refuses to provide for his family. I don't know *how* we will survive. Between Claudia's meanness and Mr. Deeters' penny-pinching, there's not an ounce of support. I'm doing all I can with the pension, but $350 per month simply can't be stretched. I suppose I could take in day care children as I did in Ohio. But sister is against it, and, to be perfectly honest, the strain of young children does harm to my fragile nerves.

4:30 One wedge white cake with coconut frosting. One sliver white cake. A few licks of extra frosting.

Feeling: Agitation. I was fully prepared to enjoy the most reasonable-sized piece of cake made by dear Michelle, and would have been able to resist the extra sliver had it not been for Sister. It is quite difficult to eat pleasantly with someone watching you. I explained the trouble with Mr. Deeters, but she was not at all sympathetic. Said I had no business bothering that "dear man" in the first place. Dear man, my left toe. He's one of the most parsimonious, least sympathetic individuals I've ever met. Sometimes I think Sister and Mr. Deeters are in cahoots just to make me miserable, I really do. They sing the same song together—money, money, money.

5:30 Three tiny pieces fried chicken, small serving mashed potatoes with a bit of gravy, extra peas and carrots. Iced tea with a dash of sugar and large lemon. Cake. Coffee with half-and-half.

Feeling: Low. Did not win lottery, although another number with 3s and 7s did. Bad luck. Sister harping on Freddy to get a job, not understanding his special nature at all. I asked Michelle for the guidance of the spirit, but alas, all souls are quiet.

8:30 Last piece of cake. Warm milk.

Feeling: Frightened. Took a nap after dinner and awoke from a terrible dream. Riding in the car down a steep and precipitous pathway. Thought Michelle was driving. Michelle is such a safe and sensible driver. Suddenly in the road ahead, saw a man swinging from a rope. I assumed it was my own dear husband, but it had somehow turned into Mr. Deeters. I shouted, Look out—you'll hit Mr. Deeters! Turned to plead with Michelle, but the driver had changed. It was Gilly. Poor, dear Gilly, driving like a maniac.

Gilly married! Even three months later, I'm still trying to get used to it. It was such a lovely wedding. But so draining! I suppose it's just extra difficult the first time you see one of your children married off, particularly in such a close-knit family as ours. Still, they gave me just enough handkerchiefs, and somehow I made it through.

Michelle is thoughtful in that way, remembering to give me my handkerchiefs. She and Sister were so busy making who knows what for the reception and tucking Gilly into her wedding gown. I had nothing to do, which is just as well—I was in such a state!

I asked Michelle if it was necessary for me to have a little talk with Gilead. My own mother gave me a little talk on my wedding day, which I can't say was particularly useful. Something about asking Rod to be gentle, and then submitting to his will. She said it was a glorious and divine act, using a voice that sounded so nervous and pained. I thought for years that the voice reflected dear mother's attitude towards the act. But now that I was facing the same task of explaining the facts of life to my daughter bride, I realized that much of the tremulousness in mother's voice must have come from embarrassment with the subject matter.

Michelle turned the question over carefully in her mind. "Perhaps Auntie could do it," she said.

"Oh, no, I really don't think, well," I told her. No. Sister simply couldn't. I'm not even certain Sister knows the subject matter (I mean, why *didn't* she and Harry ever have children?) But beyond that, Sister has no appreciation as to how to handle Gilead. She can be quite callous with the girl sometimes, shouting into her face and insisting on Gilead's participation in this or that. Gilead has always been rather delicate, especially since Rod's death. Rod was the only one who could get her to do things. But of course he spoiled her terribly, showering her with presents. She'd sit on his lap and give him kisses for each present. It was so dear.

But that was long ago and far away, as they say, when we were different people than we are now. Sometimes I think it was not just Rod who died. It was our dear little family. Of course, we had our struggles while he was still alive—money was never plentiful, and dear Rod could be a bit demanding at times. You expect that from a man, the head of the household. There was nothing wrong with it; it's perfectly reasonable for a man to expect his dinner well-cooked and on time and his children obedient and cooperative and respectful and his wife, well. I did try to be available and do all those wifely things, but childbearing took its toll—in my own way, I have as fragile health as Gilead—so it wasn't always possible. Plus it was always so unpleasant. Painful, in fact.

Oh, poor Gilead. I do hope Mr. Deeters is a gentleman; he seems to be so in the store, anyway, though he does have that nasty temper. Of course, Mr. Deeters is hardly a man like Rod. Rod was, truth be told, a bit of a bad boy. At least my family thought so. He was always chasing after those girls who dressed like gypsies, and tinkering with his car (to make it louder, my father said), and drinking outside the school dances with his buddies, greasy hair types with no ambition, my father said. I was a little surprised he courted me. The girls he dated wore lipstick to school and high heels to dances. I wasn't allowed to wear lipstick until my wedding day, and then Rod commanded me to take it off that night, along with everything else. Even my new nightgown.

Poor Gilead. I went to buy her a new nightgown. Not in Cambridge, of course. Cambridge has perfectly fine stores, mind you, but Easton is full of the wealthy retired, and their shops tend to be a bit tonier. So I slipped into a store in Easton when we went to buy the wedding gown material (these bills! They'll be the death of me) and bought it for her, pink and silky. The kind Rod used to buy her. My plan was to present it to her on her wedding day, and use it as a springboard for this discussion. She gasped when she opened the box, but would not touch it or let me speak to her, cramming her hands against her ears and shutting her eyes. Really, she can be quite stubborn at times. So she went to her wedding night with no clear idea of what to expect.

I'm sure, I'm *sure* it will be all right. Mr. Deeters is, of course, older, and well, he does strike me as a gentle man. It's just silly for me to worry. But, you see, Gilly can be so odd when she's upset. Like after Rod died.

10:30 Tiny bowl of ice cream. Two cookies. Tea with lemon and sugar.

Feeling: Tired. What a day it's been! Wonder if I've lost weight? This diet doesn't seem to be working.

Chapter 7

January 1991

GILEAD

By day, I sit by the window and wait for him. Sometimes Freddy comes over, helps to move the day towards the time my husband returns. Sometimes I make plans, big plans—a special dinner I'm going to make, a pillow slip I'm going to sew, books from his shelves I'll read so I can share his knowledge. I rarely start these projects, afraid that, like so many other times, I'll go blank, awakening hours later to find them stopped, burned, hidden. So instead, I sit by the window and wait. Something pulls me toward the night. But the night is blank, swallowed, dark. Something makes it disappear.

I long to disappear as well. Perhaps if I stare out the window long enough, I will disappear. Like father. Where is father?

RITA

I awaken nearly always in darkness. There is a man lying beside me, needy. He doesn't smell like my father, though he is old. He whispers always of his brother, his brother. The brother who went to college. The brother who had the children. The brother who is happy, content. The brother he killed. The brother.

He is angry, in bed. He whimpers in bed. He says sweet words and sucks me dry. I give and give until my skin turns inside out. I want him to stop. Words start to crawl out of my throat—Stop. Stop! I want to scream. But I am silent. I know what to do.

He does not stop, until it is over.

He does not beat me. I cower in a ball, expecting blows. He holds me gently. I feel a new feeling. It is soft and unexpected, like snow in summer. I am shaking. He is not angry; he lets me shake.

He calls for Gilly. He wants her; he does not want me. I am so angry. He wants me to pretend to be Gilly, that simpy, dopey, drainage pit of a girl. Why should I pretend to be her? And where is my father? My father wouldn't stand for this, another man in his bed. A man with so little respect for himself that he allows his woman to cry. A man who asks me what I want, as if all this fucking were for me. Who says he wants to please me. He's very mixed up. I'm supposed to please him, aren't I? All this, do you like this? Do you like to be touched there? How the hell should I know? At first I'd answer, "I want to give you pleasure." I know what I'm supposed to say. Maybe I should have said, "I want you to do it and get it over with." Ha! That woulda shocked him.

But then he'd slow down and ask, How does this feel? It felt slow. How's he ever going to finish if he goes slow? Oh, Yes! I'd say (father always likes that. Anything that agrees.) But the question throbbed through me. How does it feel?

Tingly. I told him one night, Tingly. It feels tingly. He cupped my breast, and pressed into me. My breath came in little chunks. Something deep inside was hungry. I was so afraid he'd stop. Don't stop, I whispered. He didn't. I was so surprised. What kind of man is this who lets me tell him what I want? He kissed me with his teeth; he felt angry. I'd made him angry, I'm sure. But he didn't stop. He went faster. Something was shaking inside me; a volcano. I was going to explode! I was so frightened. Stop! I told him. I was going to erupt! Stop! I begged him, but he went faster, harder, deeper. Suddenly lights appeared like prickling stars behind my eyelids. Something gushed out from me; little parts of me spewed out everywhere. The world felt liquid, and I knew that I was drowning. I looked around, terrified, and caught a glimpse of them in the mirror. There was Gilly in the corner, her back to me. Smart Lady smiled over the man's shoulder. I stared at the mirror, looking for Claw—needing Claw's protection. But he was gone. All the monsters were gone. The only thing that was left was this humping man with a tortured back. I felt him there on top of me, screaming, gushing into me with his jerking body. I couldn't help it—I started sobbing. I felt so raw, aching. He held me, stroked my back, kissed my hair. I sobbed for hours. So much of me was hurting. I'd never felt so much pain.

I'd never felt so safe.

Who is this man with pale eyes and gentle hands?

I don't think I can bear this pain. Why won't he love me? Why does he love Gilly? I want to strangle her, beat her, give her the pain. I can't bear this. Perhaps if I kill her, he'll love me instead. I must get out. I must not let sleep swallow me, as it swallowed me all those other nights. I must make him see it's me, me he wants. Rita.

NATHAN DEETERS

The marriage is not what I expected; I suppose it's never what one expects. Before the marriage I knew about Gilly's fragility —like spun sugar, sweet and easily shattered. I knew what I was taking on, or at least thought I knew. All that fragile sweetness became mine to protect, to cherish, to wrap around and succor and drink from at night. Especially at night.

At night, Gilly seems to strip down to some rawer self. What's left is something purely electric that moans and sways beneath me. I reach out to her with my desire; she hooks onto it with magnetic pull, and draws me in, a powerful sucking. Powerful for me; more and more I find myself filled with fury. All the repressions and irritations of the day surge through me as I pound myself into her receiving body and disgorge myself in her.

I didn't intend to treat her this way. In fact, my behavior frightened me at first. I don't remember this ever happening before to me. I have always been respectful of women; it's the way I was raised. When women offer you their tenderest selves (my father told me this once), we may take them as a gift, treated graciously. Secretly I supposed Gilly would be frightened of sex, especially after that first kiss. My plan was to gentle her into it. I imagined tears on our wedding night and patient explanations on my part, with slow handling before and afterwards. I did not expect this wildness, the way she tears into me, clawing and screaming. Daddy. She calls me Daddy.

At the end, I'm the one who is cradled, her quiet hands stroking my limp self. I whisper to her in the darkness, my inner doubts nesting in her thin body. She caresses my back, drawn again and again to the scar of my growth. I tell her of my brother, my twin brother—all that promise and potential swallowed up in death. She listens and strokes, a comforting cradle. "My husband, it's you who is growing," she says. "What about your promise?"

What about it? I wonder tiredly, and turn back toward her body, wishing there was some way I could stay tucked inside her all night long. "You must not do this to yourself," she tells me. "You must not fill up that hollow with self-hatred."

She doesn't understand. I didn't make the hatred.

She told me once that there are monsters inside us all, and that they hate us. I have cut the monster from me, but the hate remains.

In the morning, she treats me as though the night never came, never went. In the morning, the power of the night shuts down. Gilly retreats, tied only by gossamer threads to reality. Even the smallest practical detail seems beyond her. Simply making dinner or running the vacuum cleaner seems to overwhelm her; I'm still caring for the household as before. So any assumptions I had that Gilly would take over the housekeeping have vanished.

Yet her insights are as deep and sharply focused as any I've ever heard. Many of her seemingly casual observations about my customer's behavior have led me to make certain rearrangements in the store. I told her how people grabbed copies of anything with the royal family on the front cover, for instance. "They're fantasizing," she said. "They want to be royal. Women do that in makeup stores," she explained. So I filled the checkout aisle with makeup and perfume with royal names; ordered gourmet British-sounding food for the delicacies section; put photos of royal couples beside them. Then Gilly suggested putting magazines next to the hard-to-sell items; I tried that too. Now, women are buying as never before.

I've told her that, hoping to instill some confidence in her—perhaps a willingness to move beyond her small world by the living room window to the everyday world. I've stopped trying to get her to serve at the store; the prospect seemed to terrify her. But I've tried to interest her in other aspects of the business —the accounts, the ordering, expansion into new products. Occasionally she'll grant me a few flecks of her attention; I hook onto each effort, follow through on her suggestions and tell her the result. For example, she watched me working at my computer one night, and began asking questions. I spent several evenings explaining the intricacies of spread sheets; by the following week, she'd mastered it, and suggested several improvements. I was quite impressed.

But nothing seems to sustain her interest. I find it quite irritating. More than irritating. I find myself becoming more and more enraged. There are days—especially when Missy or Freddy shows up at the store, whining for food—when I wonder why I'm allowing myself to be leeched by this family. Then I'll go home to this woman, this child, who laughs at my descriptions of customers, delights in my recitation of the day, blankets the evening in comfortable silence and reduces me to a frenzy of hormones at night. The web closes around me again. I am trapped.

◊ ◊ ◊

I really have no clear idea what marriage is supposed to be like these days. I have no real memories of my parents' marriage; it can't have been good, else why would mother have left? I watched my friends' parents, I suppose. Jimmy's mom was one of those people who made endless cups of cocoa and grilled cheese sandwiches for us, who ironed her husband's shirts and fixed her husband's dinner and welcomed him home with a kiss on the cheek and a reminder of things he had to do that evening. But couples aren't like that nowadays, I don't think. The married women I've met have children and careers and a house they're restoring on the weekends; their husbands carry the baby in a backpack and spend their weekends sanding the stairs and stripping wallpaper. When I see these couples talking together, they're both holding out their calendars like a weapon, trying to talk the other into altering plans to fit something else in.

Gilly doesn't have a calendar. Gilly often forgets what month this is. Her only social obligation involves seeing Freddy, something that seems to be happening more and more lately. I believe the family is falling into some kind of financial difficulty, a belief that makes me want to lock up the family silver when the boy's around. Maybe I shouldn't be so suspicious; Freddy's not a bad kid. In fact, I suspect he's a lot less grimy than he seems. Gilly tells me Freddy's opinion of books occasionally, or discourses on history she claims she's heard from him. With me, all he says is Yeah or Nah or How's the car? Maybe it's a coverup. But what is he covering?

I fear what the family's financial failure could do to us. I fear what the marriage is doing to me. Most newlyweds go through an adjustment period their first year, I've been told. But I had no idea it would be this hard.

Chapter 8

January 1991

MR. DEETERS

    The biggest problem with the marriage, of course, is her family, her impossible family. Being this close to Gilly's relatives makes me feel like my own family was the epitome of normalcy. We were just your average father and son living together. Oh, I suppose it may have been a little odd to grow up without a mother. Mother left when I was quite young: five. My brother was already long dead by then, of course, though his body still crouched on my back. I have no memories of him alive. And I have only memories of memories about mother—photos I saw, vague things the neighbors said.

    Father never talked about my mother. Not true. There was the time when I was ten and wanted to join a Little League team. I was pretty good at baseball—I could catch a third base grounder and lob it to home in time for an out. And my friend Pat was joining a real team. He suggested that the two of us going in together might be a good thing. But my father had a different interpretation. Asked me what was wrong with me, wanting to go off two days a week for practice plus games. Said there'd be away games as far as Salisbury. Told me I was just restless, like my mother.

    That was the first time he'd spoken of her.

    He didn't speak of her again until my senior year in high school. I'd brought home an application to the university. I wasn't going to mention it to him, because I figured he'd be upset. My father was funny about college. Everyone says we both speak like college professors, something that always delighted him. But he never went. And I knew perfectly well that he didn't want me to go. It would mean I'd leave him, both physically and mentally. And he couldn't stand either of those.

I'd saved up $800 clerking at his grocery the previous two years, summers and after school, and figured I'd work for the rest of it. But they wanted details about my father, his job, etc. And there, at the bottom of the application, was a blank for his signature. I considered declaring myself an orphan, and weighed the odds of the university officials finding out. The odds looked good.

So I told him. He stared at me blankly, and refused to sign. I could feel him, like a web, closing around me. I said nothing. He took off his glasses, rubbed his eyes, and stared at something over my left shoulder. I wondered for years what it was—used to search the space he'd stared at that day, looking for signs. A bookcase of Reader's Digest Condensed books. A framed drawing of three ducks, one flying. (It was unclear if the duck was taking off or coming back.) A mirror, angled in such a way that he probably saw the reflected back of my head. The front door.

"So," he finally said. "You're leaving me. Just like your mother." That was the last time he mentioned her in any way.

I never left. Worked full time at his store, finally taking over when my father turned 60 and converting the place to a convenience store. I went every day, bringing home the cases of hominy and freestone peaches that my father loved until the end, five years ago. 1986. February.

I rarely looked at my father, his iron-gray hair never changing. Like the house. It wasn't until the day of his funeral that I allowed myself to really see the house, quarters of two comfortable strangers with strange hoardings. Cases of coke bottles saved against a rainy day in the basement next to the hot water heater, which had been insulated by my father during one of his periodic bouts of economy. Kitchen counters that had never been used for anything but storage, the dish drain permanently on display. Both beds neatly made. My father even made his right before his death, putting on his suit to go to the hospital. It did him no good. They stripped him of it the moment he got inside, dressing him in tubes and machines that filled him with quickening fluid while draining his dignity. He died that day for all purposes, but it took the hospital four days to stop mutilating his body and admit death.

◇ ◇ ◇

It was a house no woman could enter without wanting to change it. Until Gilly. She seems perfectly comfortable with clutter —oblivious, in fact. My father saw that few women entered at all. Oh, I know he had women, ladies he travelled to Easton and Salisbury to court and promise and leave. I found their letters in his effects—Dear Lester, when you left I realized how empty my life seems without you, I long for your comforting presence. Couldn't we meet for coffee, perhaps on the 23rd? Dear Lester, please, I don't understand what I have done that has made your feelings change so, was it the meatloaf? I will never serve it again. Dear Lester, I ache for you in the night, come to me quickly my love. The image of my father with his thick hands and graying body being ached for in the night struck me as too squalid to consider; I burned the whole collection.

I travelled farther down the road, crossing the bridge to Annapolis for theater and books and the pleasures of the body. Not until my father died did I dare to court a woman in my own home.

In the beginning it was hard to find such women. Young girls hellbent on pairing looked me over with calculator-colored eyes. I didn't look good—a hunchback still living with his father. So I began to specialize in women other men had rejected—mothers of young children with absent or ignoring husbands, disillusioned by marriage but lusting for the pleasure that the permanence of marriage could not provide. Suddenly the hump became a fascinating bit of texture. A little kindness went a very long way, I found.

The relationships began and ended in fantasy. It was their transience, their illicit nature that provided excitement. I left when they began to assume I was coming back, discussing divorce and parading their children in front of me, speaking of my paternal instincts. Asking to meet my father.

I suppose I was a cad. They were all lovely ladies with soft dresses, their pretty heads nuzzling against my neck and their hands moving under the covers with timid fingers. I treated them with gentleness until they asked for more (the most demure women could turn unbelievably passionate if they believed themselves to be naughty, I found). I was never completely dishonest, never promised anything, explained at the beginning that the circumstances of my life disallowed commitment. They probably took me on thinking they could change all that simply by being prettier, thinner, more (or less) demanding, sexier than the last one. Somewhere along the line, it all became empty. I'd look at them, and they'd become sad women with obligations and expenses. And I'd be gone.

It was in 1985, at the sour end of one of these affairs, that I returned to find my father drunk. He was perched on the living room rug, surrounded by precarious piles of books that he was rearranging on the shelves. For all his unprocessed clutter, my father had a certain compulsive tidiness to him. The spice rack was kept in alphabetical order; shoes were put away in stretchers and suits kept in garment bags. Now the bookshelves were undergoing his deranged fastidiousness.

I stood at the door, unsure how to act. He'd been drunk before — not often. Some time after his death I formed a theory that his drunken bouts were connected with women. But perhaps they were connected with me; I just don't know.

In his drunkenness, my father descended to the level of an irrational child, sure of the righteousness of his acts and in need of a great deal of coddling. They say that middle age is when you finish parenting your children and begin to parent your parents. I never had children. And that night, with my father longing for mothering from me, it began to occur to me that I'd never had parents. For if my mother abandoned me by leaving, my father abandoned me just as surely, standing between me and any deliberately chosen life I wanted to lead. His feelings for my existence—the burden I laid on him, the hole I filled for him, the rejection I symbolized for him—lay like a lead shield around the center of my life. Everything real had to be grabbed at the edges. And eventually let go.

There are things too big to be dealt with in the normal course of daily living. Truth. Love. Rage. But Lord, don't we try?

I began picking up books, putting them on dusty shelves. He cast them off, mumbling incoherently about the right order of things. I told him I was sick of the right order of things—that things deserved to find their own order, that life wouldn't fall apart if the authors weren't alphabetical, that literature deserved a certain amount of chaos. I was ramming books onto the shelves at this point, piling them in stacks. He retreated to his chair and poured himself another Jack Daniels. I picked up a book—four novels condensed to their easy-reading essence in a hardback cover—and considered throwing it at him. I imagined it hitting his head, the blood dripping down his heavy brow, spilling into those watery eyes.

"I don't know what's got into you," he said in a whiney, hurt voice. The voice only emerged in the self-pity pot of liquor. "You musta gone out and got crazy today."

"It's not today, Pop," I said. "It's not even this year. It's my whole fucking life." The words drained my arm; I dropped the book. It thudded onto the pine floor.

"Seems to me you got a pretty good life," he began. "Good job, roof over your head, plenty of food on the table." He focused on the floor. "Good books," he added. "What's missing?" he asked, genuinely puzzled.

"Everything," I told him, and went to pour myself a drink. Not from his bottle. I brought vodka from my room and splashed it onto two foggy ice cubes in an old jelly jar.

When I came back, he appeared to be sinking into his chair, the glass of Jack Daniels lending shape to his hand. His hand was the only part of his body that still had stiffness; everything else sloped and slumped. "Seems to me when I was your age I felt like that," he said. His hand shook with age, the drink sloshing chaotically in the glass. It had an appearance of merriment that struck me as out of place. "Course, I was burdened with a child, so maybe I just felt I didn't have the freedom to look for more. But I tell you son, you're wasting your time. There ain't nothing more. And that's the sad truth."

"You're wrong," I told him, draining my glass. I could feel the ice gone smooth and clean, clanking up against my teeth. The vodka burned pleasantly in my throat. Of course, I believed my father. Or perhaps I was afraid to find out if he was wrong.

We never spoke of it again.

I never spoke of it to anyone, not even to my brother's grave where I went each month to put such musings as these. Until Gilly. She was holding a cup of tea one November evening, after we'd been married about two months. For some reason—perhaps the stiffness in her hand as she cradled the cup while the rest of her body curved with the chair—it reminded me of that scene. So I told it to her, pouring it into her liquid eyes. She began to cry, which alarmed me. "I'm sorry," I told her. "I didn't mean to upset you."

She stared at her tea, clutching it with both hands now. "It's not you," she said, her voice so soft and high I could barely hear it. Then she looked at me. She was still in pain. I guess I expected pity, and steeled myself to reject it and all its humiliating condescension. But I didn't see pity. Only a sense of connectedness—a line drawn from her pain to mine. "Your mother," she began. I must have winced; I didn't want to hear this. Too many women had made pronouncements on my mother, and all the ways they were going to save me from her desertion, the poor orphan boy. "You just need some mothering," they'd tell me, fluffing my pillow in beige motel rooms, scrubbing my back with tiny slivers of packaged soap. I didn't want this from Gilly too. I thought, I hoped she was different.

Gilly stopped, and traced the rim of her tea cup. Her leg started to swing. She could see I couldn't bear it. That made me furious—this fragile girl from a grimy family forebearing my feelings. "Say it," I told her.

She looked up and sighed, opening her mouth. "Your mother left because she could not bear her life," she said, the words coming out like water from a pump, flowing furiously from her mouth to the space between us. "And your father stayed because he could not bear his. You were expected to bear it for the both of them." I stared at her. I didn't know what to think.

"They're dead," I reminded her.

She looked at me and smiled, a quirky smile. "I wish you'd thrown that book," she said.

◊ ◊ ◊

This is all I can remember about what happened next. I was already stunned by her words about my parents; the rest of her words took days to register. I'm still not sure what they mean. Perhaps they mean nothing.

I reached out and took her hand. "Gilly," I said.

"Gilly's gone," she said. "Anyway, you don't want Gilly. She can't do anything for you." She leaned over, tilted her head, and looked at me. "You probably want Rita."

"What are you talking about?" I asked.

She looked down at my pants. I followed her glance. She could see my desire bursting out. "Yeah, you want Rita. I'll put her in the bedroom." With that, she stopped swinging her leg, stood up, and walked to the bedroom, her body held ramrod straight. Halfway there her body seemed to change, loosen. Her hips began to swing. I focused on her round little rump, and smiled.

I took her teacup and mine into the kitchen and rinsed them in the sink. Then I reached into the cupboard and poured myself three fingers of vodka. No ice. And tried to consider what I'd just heard. My mind numbed to nothingness.

Then, a fragment appeared. Just a feeling I got sometimes in dreams—of long, wavy hair drifting across my face, and something small and wet splashing onto my cheek. "Goodbye, my beloved," says the voice, my mother's voice. I'm afraid; but I cannot awaken.

The fragment is gone. I am standing by the sink; the glass is empty. I'm always shaken when this image comes. I wait for the shaking to pass.

I turn off lights, lock the door, walk into my bedroom. Our bedroom now. The light is off; moonlight glints through a crack in the curtain. Gilly is on her side, turned toward the curtain. The moonlight lies casually across her naked body, like the arm of a lover. I disrobe, hang up my clothes, put the underclothes in the hamper. I turn to face my wife; my child. She's caressing patterns on the sheets with one finger. I climb onto the bed, roll her toward me. She smiles, her fingers reaching for the hair on my chest. I lie on top of her; her legs spread to receive me. My arm locks around her under her neck. My other hand comes up to her face, cups around her cheek. She's tucking my cock inside her. My heart stops; I hear myself moan. I hate myself for needing her so much. I can feel her power over me; want to smash it.

I press my face to her, first the lips, then the teeth, then the tongue. I'm going to devour her. She gasps; she's frightened, shaking. I don't care; I want her. I'm thrusting into her, hard, deep. I can't stop. I want to split her open. My teeth travel down her chin, gnaw on her neck. She's squealing; she's in pain. I thrust deeper, harder. I'm going to break her apart, pull out her organs and eat them. My head is filling up with noise. Words, I hear old words, words in a woman's voice, my mother's voice: Goodbye, Lester, the words say, shout, scream, Goodbye you bastard, goodbye, goodbye. I don't want to hear it, I don't want to hear it! I push out the noise, furious. I push up on my arms to get more leverage, and slam into this woman as hard as I can. She's begging me to stop; I can see tears on her cheeks in the moonlight. My abdomen is moving with a compulsive fury, like waves in a storm. I cannot stop; nothing can stop me—I will possess her; I will entrap her; I will pin her down and hold her captive. She reaches her hands up, strokes my face to soothe me, slow me. I pull her hands down over her head, pin her down, turn my head away so I won't see that face, drowning in tears. The words return, pick up where they left off—You gonna take the boy? I hear my father, screeching. You at least gonna take this goddamn kid? I hear myself screaming, feel the agony inside Gilly, her muscles expanding around me. All of me pumps into her; I'm trapped there. I collapse, panting, exhausted. Everything is black. There is only noise of breathing, and somewhere beneath me, a child crying.

I held her all night, so afraid that she'd leave me for what I'd done. At dawn, little licks of sunrise light came in and were spattered by the dresser mirror. It made tiny shards of light on the bedspread, sharpened silently as the sun rose.

I'm so afraid. First she'll know me, then she'll come to despise what she knows. And then she'll leave me with nothing but mirrors to reflect my own self.

The sunlight grew and softened, leaving everything visible, dusty, ugly. I glanced down at the tangled hair of my sleeping wife; passed my own hand in front of the mirror. I saw it there, the part of me that lives, trapped in reflection. It was the hand of an aging monster, freed at last of all constraints but time and gravity.

I glanced back at my wife. She always leaves me, I realized. She's right—Gilly is gone, or going, most of the time. Who is this child in my arms?

Chapter 9

January 1991

MISSY

Catastrophe! We are dangling over the very precipice of existence! Where will we go from here?

I take my pen in hand (actually, it's auntie's pen—mine has disappeared somewhere) to write a saving chapter for this family's exploits. It must involve gathering *large quantities of money*. Auntie says we must pay our own way, or she will throw us out into the snow! Well, not snow exactly—it doesn't snow nearly so often here as it does in Ohio, but I can't imagine anyone as cruel and exacting as Auntie throwing us out until there's a good foot of the stuff on the ground. She must mean to wait for a blizzard. I'm praying for global warming.

I returned to watching "Day's Turnings" which I have recently decided has a more worthy expression of the fictional soul, despite reception (Auntie will not spring for a satellite dish, the old tightwad), looking for some glimmer of a suggestion for a way out of this dilemma. But really, these plots pale next to real life. So little imagination. The lottery, bestowed frequently on these characters, is unlikely to fall on us (I mean, good heavens, even Mother tries that). And while the possibility of unexpected inherited wealth seems to fit the bill, so to speak, mother assures me we've already drained dry all known relatives, dead and otherwise. Sometimes I think I could do a far better job of writing than is found on these television screens. Simply transcribing my family—sans editorial—would complete the task.

THE PERILOUS GRASONS

Cinncinnati, Ohio, was the site of my birth—a difficult delivery accomplished in two stages near and in an imposing and impersonal hospital. Mother had longed to enter the hospital earlier, playing out those last tedious months in the comparative comfort of a sterilized room. But there was no money nor anyone to relieve her of the responsibility of an active and often destructive two-year-old boy, and the doctor assured her that lying in her own bed at home would accomplish the same thing. She gained 60 pounds, on top of the twenty or so extra ones laid on by the onset of Freddy. She says she spent those months watching soap operas, which perhaps explains my kinship with these tortured souls. Gilly must have hovered in back, and thus did not become tuned to the TV life.

The labor was vivid torture, mother says, but she failed to act on it. Mother tends to panic in crises, leaving those moments to stronger souls. She intended to turn this call to action over to her husband, but father had stopped by a local tavern on his way home, as was his wont, to engage in genial conversation, and thus missed this call to duty. Mother finally asked for help from an elderly neighbor, who climbed into his bathrobe and slippers to provide transportation. His nervousness over her outbursts of rhythmic pain caused him to run several red lights, resulting in an unfortunate accident—the effects of which did nothing to slow the labor. Perhaps I felt called to duty, for by the time the police arrived on the scene, my head was nudging at mother's portal, so to speak, and I was delivered in the backseat by an uninstructed police officer who assured mother that he did it without looking at her privates.

Gilly, of course, had it easier—she always lets me be the pioneer. Her arrival took place in the competent surroundings of the emergency room, with masked personnel cutting the cord and wrapping her in recently washed swaddling clothes. Still, she was a tiny, fragile baby, separated from me into the intensive care unit for a day until lifted by my father, who said we had no money for such things.

That must have been when their special bond developed. Gilly wasn't so much fretful as limp (I was the squawker, Mother says), and required hours of cradling. Mother says father sang Gilly into life, carrying her for hours while he hummed old camp songs, stroking her tiny body and paying rapt attention to her toilette.

Many of my friends have asked me over the years, Michelle, aren't you jealous of Gilly? All that attention she got from father—taking her with him to the tavern in her pram, strolling with her to the hardware, and in later years, when his job required so much travel, plumping up pillows for her in the front seat of the Chevy where she waited with her coloring books while he made his sales, and cuddling with her at night in his Econo Motel room. She'd come back from these trips with a fresh box of crayons and one of those garish all-day suckers, while we'd get Where's-my-supper questions and tedious arguments about money.

But no, I didn't begrudge it to Gilly. She was, after all, a fragile soul (as mother reminded us), and helped to keep father in line (he did drink, truth be told, a bit too much). And she never looked very happy after those trips—just tired and out of sorts. She'd want to go off to bed or play with her dolls, but father would insist that she come pour the cream in his coffee or fetch his slippers or play beside him so he could stroke her hair while he watched sports shows on TV. Freddy would stare in sullen silence beside him, arms folded, ignoring his homework, while I worked on my social studies or baked for mother. Mother got so little attention. Really, it was pitiable the way a plate of brownies could brighten her anxious evenings. I suppose it was about that period when mother moved into my bedroom—her sleep was fretful and she required much comforting, which father was of course too worn out or absent to give. So Gilly moved into the master bedroom in mother's stead. We thought nothing of it at the time; it was the most reasonable thing to do. Only Freddy, with his mean mind, made any comment. He actually had the nerve to suggest there was something unwholesome about it. Father belted him, of course. And as for mother and I, I'm happy to say that Freddy's comment fell on deaf ears.

Things were actually looking up for us just before father died.

Oh, I know Freddy was involved with that dreadful motorcycle gang where we all knew he didn't belong—especially father. Especially after the earring incident (Freddy looked quite ludicrous in a skull-and-crossbones earring). Freddy has never been willing to admit his intelligent side, hiding behind his sarcasm and his Oh, yeahs and his leather jacket. Still, I think he was planning to go to college—I found catalogs for the state schools in his room.

And things were looking up for mother, too. She'd had some success selling her little hints and diets to Ladies Day and Contemporary Women, which brought in extra money. I was able to run the household by then, despite the headaches which so often besieged me. And father must have been doing well as he traveled far and wide. Gilly roomed with us (she was in high school, after all) when he left, except in summer. I believe father looked forward to the summers, traveling with Gilly. Poor dear, I suppose he got rather lonely on the road.

Then in the summer of her 17th year, Gilly refused to go. She sought summer jobs—probably as an excuse—but was unable to obtain one. There were families that hired her for babysitting, however, and she would line up jobs for those weeks when father was to be away. He was quite distressed about it, as I recall, and even more distressed to discover she'd been dating while he was gone. Actually, she'd been dating for some time (boys liked her for some elusive reason), but disguised it by meeting her dates at the Mall. Even I, her twin, was unaware, although Freddy later said he knew (apparently some contemporary of his teased him about having "the easiest piece at Franklin High" for a sister. I assume Freddy throttled him. Freddy is big on fights. I don't know why. Father practically broke his hand punishing the boy for fighting in elementary school.)

Gilly must have been feeling more daring that summer, however, because the dates started showing up at the house—boys in loud cars and greasy hair. Oh, mother fussed, but Gilly just slipped her feet into high-heeled sandals and stomped out.

I suppose Mother decided to speak to father about it at the end of one of his long trips. She showed her usual sense of timing—not waiting for the end of a day or two of good meals and comfortable sleep, but plunging right in before the daze of travel had left his eyes. Gilly had not come home for dinner, something that had been happening more and more frequently (the truth is that she didn't come home at all some nights, but Freddy covered for her the few times mother asked), so perhaps that was the heat that boiled mother's pot. In any event, by the time Gilly arrived looking disheveled and (I hate to admit this, but fiction requires truth) a little drunk, father was in a rage. He insisted that she drop her pants right there for a spanking, grabbing her when she attempted to run. I could see father was losing—he was middle-aged by then, after all—so I grabbed her arms to help him. Freddy ran over, shouting my name. I thought he'd come to lend assistance, but he quite strangely started trying to pull me off of Gilly. Mother was no help at all, choosing this moment to clean the silverware drawer in the kitchen.

Oh, the drama! Father and Freddy got into a physical tussle while I attempted to hold Gilly. I'm not sure what happened between the males, only that Freddy roared off on his motorcycle, but he was home next day with a broken nose. I saw him. By then, of course, father was dead, and to this day I don't know what scars his body bore from the fight.

I think—oh, I must confess this, despite how it tears at my soul—it would have been all right if I could have held Gilly. Then father could have re-established his authority in a normal way, and the girl would have had some sense whipped into her. But she bit me—badly (the scar is still quite vivid on my hand), and I let go.

She ran upstairs to her room and was packing—perhaps intending to run away?—when father broke down the door. Father was a bit out of control by that time, with these two wretched children questioning his authority in such blatant ways. I remember Gilly screaming that she'd tell. Tell what? That she was an undisciplined teenager requiring and receiving punishment? Just who did she think would care?

Father called for the rope (Gilly frequently had to be tied in those days to be punished, she was so big) and I brought it, volunteering to help. He gagged her, which certainly helped dim that awful screaming, but she looked at me with terrible eyes. She can be quite mean sometimes. A real monster.

I've given a great deal of thought to the rope, that terrible rope. Dear reader, I hope you understand that I never would have brought it, not for one second, if I'd known he was going to turn it on himself in that hideous way. I thought he was simply going to tie Gilly to the bed. Perhaps he did, for they found rope burns the next day on her wrists and ankles. Then again, they found rope burns on father's wrists as well. Gilly was mute by that time, and for some time to come. We found her huddling in the corner. She had her knees pulled up to her chin to cover herself. As usual, she was unclothed—you'd think she'd at least have had sense enough to put some clothes on.

Father had put his clothes back on. He was hanging by his neck from a hook that had been pounded into the ceiling months earlier. We hadn't gone in. Mother hadn't even checked, though I did, briefly. I saw only a hanging shadow in the mirror. I assumed it was Gilly; father liked to string her up sometimes as a punishment, using that pulley he had for stringing up dead deer.

So I didn't go in; I waited downstairs for father to finish with Gilly and come down. It was Freddy, his nose caked with blood from the night before, who cut our father down.

◊ ◊ ◊

The judge declared it a simple case of suicide, finding Gilly not guilty of any charges, though he highly recommended that she be retained in the hospital to which she'd been sent that first month. But the hospital quickly discovered that we were in no position to pay even that first month's bill, and agreed with our conclusion that Gilly would be better served by staying in the bosom of her loving family. Personally, I wish the judge could have left at least a slight space for doubt—perhaps the insurance company would have been willing to pay some amount (father had quite a large policy).

The hospital recommended that Gilly see a psychiatrist on the outside for treatment. They had a lot of fancy terms to describe her, and wanted to know more about her childhood. But I agreed with mother that we needed no such people poking their noses into our family's business. Besides, we'd never had insanity in our family, and we certainly weren't going to allow it to start now.

Still and all, I would have been happier with a verdict of murder by reason of insanity. That way the state would have paid to institutionalize Gilly. And we would have gotten our insurance. It wouldn't have been unfair. I mean, there's every chance Gilly did kill him. Or perhaps Freddy killed him, though that's a separate issue. Freddy quite unfairly says that I had a hand in it, claiming that he saw me lift something from the room before the police were called. Well, of course I took things. I didn't want the police thinking we were untidy. And no, I didn't put them back. Once father was dead, there was no need for those things anymore.

I wonder if "Day's Turnings" would pay for this story?

I wonder if Mr. Deeters is insured?

Chapter 10

March 1, 1991

FREDDY

This is the end of our second winter on the eastern shore. Winters are a hell of a lot more bitter here than they were in Ohio. The land's so flat, with nothing but these stubborn pines and chicken farms to stop the wind. The whole place looks to me like a furry table gouged by some lesser god with a fork fetish. The ice starts building in December, cracking and splitting whenever the sun comes out, but then building up again. By now in March, the ice has gotten so tricky that the natives—except the boatmen; nothing stops them—are all squirreled inside for good with nothing to do, and only chattering on the telephone to keep them alive.

I believe that malice is the last thing to die in us. Winter seems to strip people down to it. The last tacky threads of Christmas decoration are torn down from the porchlights, and all that's left in us is bitterness and gossip.

Mostly over my family, I suspect. My family is the sort that sticks out even in a place like Cincinnati. There was no hope of hiding out in Cambridge—Missy (and even mother) must have known that. But we flung ourselves here anyway, falling on the mercies of Auntie (such as they are) and becoming fresh meat for the wide eyes of Cambridge.

I still visit Cambridge a couple of times a week. God knows why—my girlfriend, Cheri, acts like it's some sort of psychological defect. I go to see Gilly, I guess. At first it looked like I was going to move in with Gilly when Auntie threatened to throw us out. Gilly started putting my stuff in the extra bedroom, and occasional dinners there became occasional overnights, followed by whole weekends. But Deeters stopped it by arranging this job at a station toward Annapolis where he goes to get his car fixed. I'd tinkered with his car a few times—it was something to do—and he praised me to the skies to Mike, his mechanic. Which was a nice thing to do, in a way, though I know he didn't do it to be nice—he did it to get me out of his hair.

Anyway, I moved across the bridge to a little apartment in yuppieville, and now spend my days getting greasy for college-educated dollars. I suppose I shouldn't envy the yups. We could have gone to college. My grades weren't nearly as bad as you'd expect, considering how little time I spent working for them. And God knows Missy could have had her pick of colleges. Even Gilly could have gone if she'd found a college that just required gobs of reading. In fact, I kind of hoped that after the death and the bad period that followed, she might go. It would have gotten her away from the family. Even moving to Cambridge I thought might be a start for her. Even marrying Deeters.

I'm starting to find out stuff about Deeters. It's not like I'm looking for it—people just tell me. One weekend this last November, for instance, I literally smashed into some information.

I'd sauntered down to the Texaco station to look for Jack. He's about the best guy in Cambridge with cars. He knows nothing about foreign cars, though—says they all have names that sound like karate yells, with engines to match. But a carburetor is a carburetor, and the bus was acting up.

Greg was there, pumping gas on Sunday. Jack had taken the day off. But Greg said he knew a little about carburetors—he'd rebuilt one for his third Chevy. He's got a Ford now. Other guys go through women at about the same clip as Greg goes through cars; he says cars are cheaper.

I was just suggesting that he drop by the house after work when this old guy rolls up in his pickup. He's got his Sunday shirt on, but I can see he's been hitting the bottle in mortal and off-scheduled sin. Musta bought it Saturday night (they're strict around here). He's there for gas and a pack of cigarettes. I was sitting in the office because it was cold outside, so I watched him trying to put skinny quarters into that tiny slot. "You're new, ain'tcha?" he asks. I'm trying not to laugh at his stubby fingers missing the hole.

"Actually, I don't work here. I'm just waiting for Greg."

"Live around here?" he asks. Plunk—a quarter swallowed.

"Yessir," I said. Pa was big on yessirs. It works wonders with the irrational, I've noticed.

"Just moved here, I bet."

"No, sir. We've been here almost two years now." Old fart.

Plunk. Thonk. Slide. He reached down to get his Kools, and looked out. "That your bus?" he asks.

"Yessir."

"You must be one of the Bunting kids," he says.

"Grason. We live with Mrs. Bunting." That's my aunt.

"Grason. Say—I know you. You're the one whose sister married the hunchback, ain'tcha?"

I smiled serenely. "Pardon me?"

"Aw, don't take no offense. Nate's a nice enough guy. And your sister must be something. Half the widows and divorcees in the county been trying to land him for years. Say, how old is she anyway?"

"What did you call Mr. Deeters?" I was trying to sound stern.

"I didn't mean nothing. That's jes his nickname, on account of the hump." I must have looked confused, for he said, "but I guess you don't know about that, do you? Course not. He had it off, musta been, oh, four or five years ago. Made him look much better. Can't say it did much for his personality, though. Seems to me he's gotten real snippy since he lost his hump. Almost like all the kindness in him got cut out with it. But maybe your sister will put that back in, eh?" he said, leering blearily towards me. "Nothing like a good woman in your bed, huh?"

And that's when I tried to punch him. Fortunately, Greg showed up just in time to block the punch. I'm glad he did. That old fart wasn't worth a night in jail.

◇ ◇ ◇

That was my first real piece of evidence that there's something deformed about Deeters. Other than his willingness to marry into our family, I mean. And all that bit about ESP and psychic twins and stuff. I thought he was just odd. Now I'm not sure.

Here's something else I found out about him. For all I know, it's something everyone in Cambridge knows except us (we're the source—not the confidante—of gossips). But Cheri said he'd made a fuss (that I believe) of keeping it secret. She's a nurse with a 1979 VW beetle I keep alive with pirated parts, and a body I keep going with buttered popcorn and lots of T.L.C. She only told me this, she says, because I'm a member of the family.

Anyway, it seems that the hunchback wanted to have the hump taken off a few years back, when Cheri was working surgery up at Johns Hopkins in Baltimore. Came in to have it looked at. Why he hadn't gone earlier, I can't imagine. Cheri said it had something to do with his father forbidding it. Anyway, they did all those tests and pokes and probes, and decided it was safe and necessary and covered by insurance to remove the hump.

Here's the weird part. Deeters thought the hump was his brother. He thought he was a twin who'd formed around his brother. Isn't that bizarre?

Cheri said the doctors were mixed about it. They did pull something off of him that might have been the remains of an unborn fetus. Then again, it might have just been a weird-shaped growth. But Deeters was absolutely positive it was his brother. Said his father had told him that it was. Said they'd had it x-rayed when he was just a little thing, though he didn't know who'd taken the x-rays. Insisted that the hospital give him the remains from the hump. And—get this—had them buried. In a grave.

That just gives me the creeps. I wonder if Gilly knows about the grave? I don't want to tell her—it's just so weird. On the other hand, Gilly is about the one person in the world who wouldn't be weirded out by it. I mean, she's buried a lot of strange stuff in her time too. I don't mean things, or people, exactly. I mean like memories. Gilly—the one I call Gilly, anyway—doesn't seem to know anything about what happened with father. Not even the stuff I knew, we all knew, about what father was doing to her. She always acted—acts— like he was a regular dad, like everybody else's.

I don't blame her, exactly. I mean, who'd want to remember all that stuff? Still, I wonder sometimes what all this forgetting costs Gilly. It's not like she doesn't remember, and therefore has this great life. It's like she doesn't remember, and is only half-there most of the time. A sliver of a person. Like the silent half of her—the part that knows, that must know—has eaten her up.

◊ ◊ ◊

I wonder if Gilly even knows about the hump. I wonder how much Gilly knows about her husband. I think she likes him. God knows why. He spends loads of time fussing at her to do things—a habit I assumed she'd have squashed by now with her lack of action—but she seems to make at least a plodding, half-hearted effort to do a small portion of his bidding, occasionally. And she talks more. Especially while she's driving.

You read that right—Gilly's driving now. It was one of Deeters' more bizarre commands, an idea so completely insensitive, I thought maybe Deeters had some kind of brain tumor when it came to Gilly. Gilly froze, of course. Then she took protective action. She told me about it. That meant I was to stop Deeters. (Freddy sweeps up.)

I drove over to the store, trying to work out a plan. It's been pointed out to me by more than one woman that I tend to bang into arguments head first (or fist first, as the case may be). Beating up an almost 40-year-old man who supplies my family with groceries in full view of the customers of Cambridge seemed a little stupid. I thought about how Missy would handle it, but didn't have a sob story or a dangling sword I could hold over Deeters (this was before I knew about the hunchbrother). I decided on a tack I've rarely taken, simply for the shock value. I decided to go man to man with him. Hard to imagine, given both characters.

Deeters was ringing up candy bar sales for the afterschool crowd, so he couldn't talk. But he mentioned a problem with his brakes, so I moseyed out back to tinker with it. I was going to plan my speech as I diddled around back there. But I found something strange: A hole had been punched that drained the brake fluid. I stood there trying to decide what had done this. Or who. And if I wanted to be the one to tell Deeters. Finally I decided to tell him that the car needed a part and not to drive it until I could get it for him.

At 4:30, Joel Tilghman and Juney May Brighton took over for Deeters at the counter. He ambled outside into the December air, and asked about his car. I told him about the new part as casually as I could. Then I stood up, looked him in the eye and said, "we need to talk about Gilly. She said you want her to take driving lessons."

"Ah, yes, ahem, I've been meaning to talk with you about that, Freddy," he said. He has? I wondered. "Yes. Yes," he continued, probably checking this off his to-do list. "I believe it would be best if you taught her." I must have looked surprised. "I'll pay you, of course. It's just that these driving schools are so, well, I mean, I imagine Gilly might find them a little—what is the word?—intimidating. Yes, that's it. Intimidating."

I saw that his search for this latent vocabulary lesson had completely blinded him to the obvious. "Gilly can't possibly learn to drive," I said, showing him the elephant in front of his nose.

"No?" he said, focusing.

"No," I stated. "It's far too dangerous for her and everyone else on the road. That is, assuming she had the courage to even turn the key. The whole idea's ridiculous."

He looked at me sadly, a pitiful smile on his face. "Sometimes, Freddy," he said, with words that sounded as if they were carefully chosen (but weren't), "I think the whole family grossly underestimates Gilly's capabilities." My hands clenched. "Except you," he added hastily. "I thought perhaps you—of all of them," here he gestured carelessly towards the road leading home, "understood her depth."

"I do understand her," I said through teeth cracked open just wide enough to emit sound. "Which is why I know how crazy it is to put her through trying to learn to drive."

"Gilly is a beautiful blossom," he said in his flowery way. "Each petal opens singly, a moment at a time. We must give her warmth and encouragement and opportunity to open."

Gilly is a flower blighted by sudden and relentless heat, I thought, whose best hope is sheer survival. "I ain't teaching her to drive," I said.

"It will give her freedom," he said.

"What it will give is someone to run your errands," I told him.

"That will give her purpose, which she sorely needs. Gilly is destined to do far more than fading by the window. She should never have been allowed to collapse on herself like this."

"Allowed!" Both hands were clenched and straining at my jacket pocket. "ALLOWED!"

"Well, perhaps that's not the best word. And I'm sure you all thought you were doing your best by her. But now she must be given the chance to come out of herself. Driving is an important first step," he said.

Count to ten, I told myself. Count to ten, and then hit him. "It wasn't us who hurt Gilly," I said as steadily as I could, though my voice was choking.

Deeters did the wrong thing then. He gave me a look, a long look. It was pity. Taking a step toward me, he put his arm on my shoulder and said, "Freddy, I didn't mean. . . ."

"I ain't giving Gilly no fucking driving lessons, understand me?" I shouted. "And neither is anybody else!" Jumping on my bike, I flew off toward Annapolis.

But of course I was back the next day to take care of that car.

◊ ◊ ◊

I was wrong about the driving lessons, though. After I fixed the car, I stayed away a couple, three weeks, trying to cool off. Then I showed up when I knew the condescending bastard would be nowhere around. Gilly looked like she'd been waiting for me, standing by the door. She used to do that, even as a little kid. It was as if she always knew when anyone was coming home. "You here for my lesson?" she asked, right off.

I was thrown by the question. "We don't hafta do that," I told her. "I squared it with Deeters."

Then Gilly did something even stranger than talking. She looked disappointed. She opened her mouth to speak a couple of times, then sat down, closing her eyes. A minute later, she opened them, looked around carefully, started swinging her leg and said "Hi, Freddy!" in a squeaky voice.

I grinned. "Hey, Smart Lady," I said. "How you been?"

"Been good," she said. "You gonna teach us to drive?"

"You wanna?" I asked. I really wanted to talk with her; maybe a long drive would keep her around.

"Rita really wants to," she told me. "You go get the Volvo; I'll tell Rita." She got up and walked into the bedroom.

By the time I got back from the store (getting the keys from Deeters meant listening to an this endless lecture on using the back roads and making sure everyone had seatbelts on and not stopping on any hills the first lesson), Gilly—sorry, Rita—was dressed and ready to go. Where she got that outfit, I don't know—a red V-necked sweater that was a couple sizes too tight, and black leather pants. I quickly discovered that the fine points of driving were totally lost on her; her interest was in going as fast as possible, especially around curves. She loved switching gears, grinding them as loudly as she could and squealing around corners. I took her out on Rt. 50 so she could do a fast stretch; we made it to Easton in 10 minutes, which is saying something.

Lessons were fun. We discovered every narrow road in Talbot county, where Rita tested the car's ability to do 90 or more. Then she asked for something more challenging—a trip over the bridge to my apartment. I thought at first that she just wanted to see where I'd settled. But as soon as she hit the Bay Bridge, I could see it was the challenge of that barrier that was important to her. She was really scared of the bridge—just like mother. But she was determined not to give in to her fear. Sometimes she'd reach the other side of the bridge, unhinge her white knuckles from the wheel, turn the car around, and go back over. Gradually, she could do it without going white. I was glad. I'll admit it was a little tough sitting in the passenger seat while she stiff-armed herself over the bridge the first dozen or so times. But it proved to me what I've always known about my sister—that she's got a lot of courage. More than me. Maybe more than anyone in the family.

After she'd conquered the bridge, she'd just show up every once in awhile in Annapolis, helping herself on the way to a coke from the station's vending machine and smiling shyly at my boss. He liked her; she was easy to tease. And sometimes she'd bring him little presents—apple butter she'd made, or a notice from the newspaper of some contest (my boss is crazy about contests).

Sometimes when she showed, my boss would give me a couple of hours off to go driving. We'd tootle around Annapolis so Gilly could get used to driving in traffic. Or I'd take her from there to this crab house in Cambridge so she could buy oysters for Deeters and crab cakes for me (the big perk of living on the Eastern shore is crab cakes). While I chowed down, she'd steal half my french fries unless I told her I wanted to talk with Smart Lady. Smart Lady was easy to get out now—I'd just bring her a coke, and Smart Lady would come out to drink it. Then she'd start swinging her leg and looking at the crab pots hanging from the ceiling, smiling.

It was like the old days. I'd tell her about all my girl troubles, and the cars I was rebuilding, and gossip about my nutty boss (he spent all his money on those contests, and would turn up with new refrigerators and miniature TVs, grinning).

She had nice things to say about Deeters. Said he was patient with Gilly, and tender with Rita.

"He got any enemies?" I asked her, smearing tartar sauce on my crab cake. You gotta try one; they're incredible.

"Don't think so," she said, swigging her coke. "He's sharp in business—he doesn't take any excuses from anyone. But he's not dishonest, if that's what you mean. Why do you ask?"

"Someone's trying to hurt him," I said, telling her about the drained brake fluid. She looked thoughtful, swinging her leg and occasionally stirring her coke with her finger. She'd been talking so much, I forgot about not pushing her. "Whatcha thinking?" I asked. I shouldn't have.

"Missy. Or Rita," she whispered.

"Rita?" I asked. That didn't square with the Rita I knew. "Why the hell would Rita do it?"

Smart Lady looked troubled. "Rita doesn't understand that she's just...that she and Gilly are..."

"The same person," I said.

Smart Lady looked at me evenly. "They're not the same person, Freds," she said. "And that's what drives Rita nuts. Deeters thinks he's married to Gilly, and Rita wants him to ask for her. She's jealous."

I guess I musta squirmed; this stuff makes me really uncomfortable. Something else was making me even more uncomfortable, though, and I felt I had to talk to her about it. "Tell me something," I began. "You don't suppose...I mean, could Claw be out to get Deeters for some reason?"

Smart Lady looked startled. "What makes you say that?"

"Well, I mean, it was Claw who was out the night father died, right?"

Smart Lady went rigid, and dropped her coke. She closed her eyes and started shaking as it smashed to the floor.

I didn't know which to clear up first—the coke, or my sister. Freddy sweeps up. I cleaned the floor.

When I looked up, Gilly was back, her haunted eyes scanning frantically around the room. "It's okay, sweetheart," I told her. "I cleaned it up." She stared at me, puzzled. "If you get Smart Lady, I'll get her another," I said, hoping to get things back to where they were.

She moved her mouth into a question: Who?

"Remember Smart Lady?" I asked. This was so freaky.

Gilly shook her head, No.

I sighed. "Let's go," I told her, pulling her toward the car. As I drove her back through the frozen, flat land, I heard her humming nursery rhymes to herself.

Chapter 11

July 1991

NATHAN DEETERS

Claudia herself came to the store today, asking if I could speak with her privately. I steered her to the back room, steeling myself for her words. She said she was considering going to the police to ask them to remove her sister and niece, both of whom steadfastly refuse to gain employment. I told her I was unfamiliar with the law in these cases, and suggested she phone Harry Blackwell; he's been useful to me in a couple of sharp deals wholesalers have tried to put over on me.

It is wholly unlike her to even consider bringing the police into family business; she must be at her wit's end. Still, I couldn't bring myself to encourage her to action; God knows what ramifications it will bring on Gilly. Missy has a devious mind; I imagine she'll move heaven and earth to get me to take over her family's support. Groceries are one thing; taking over the Grasons' expenses is simply beyond tolerance. But I hate to see Gilly being squeezed between Missy and me. She's fragile enough as it is.

I must say I was unprepared for the depth of Gilly's mental problems. That's what they are; I need to face it. I suppose I must have known before I married her how tentative her grasp on reality was. But she seemed to perk up, slowly last fall, steadily this winter. The driving lessons helped a great deal, as I knew they would. That gave her a certain amount of a freedom to explore the area, as well as a certain confidence in herself. There were other signs of health: She bought new software for the computer and redid the inventory system, for example. And instead of just talking about my customers, she began making specific suggestions about the business. It all proved quite useful. Brought a fresh eye to the place.

But then sometime towards the end of winter, Freddy brought her home from a driving lesson. She'd gone limp, and continued to spiral into some sicker self. The person I've been coming home to since early summer is a child who spends her day coloring with crayons, drawing frightening pictures on the back of used computer sheets.

And then there are the nightmares.

◇ ◇ ◇

The first one actually came in April. I was disturbed by it, of course. In fact, it woke me out of a sound sleep. But I didn't think too much about it again until summer, when each night seemed to bring on another, more drastic vision.

The wail that broke my sleep in spring seemed to come from someone much younger than my wife. We'd fallen asleep after lovemaking, enfolded in each other's arms, with Gilly's fingers entwined in my chest hair—a position I'd become accustomed to over the months. Gilly seems to find my chest hair reassuring in some strange way; I've awoken occasionally to find her cradled next to it, sucking her thumb.

That night she shot up in bed, her body jerking with a power all its own, and screamed about a rope. I reached out and pulled her to me; she jerked backwards, pounding on my chest. "Gilly, it's me, your husband," I told her, but she moaned like a wounded animal and would not be touched. Finally I turned on the reading light. She was hunched in the corner of the bed, rubbing her wrists and weeping. When I finally got her attention, she reached her hands out to me, palms up. I looked, and looked again. In that strange, deep night, with sleep fogging my brain, I seemed to see raw marks on her wrists. "The rope," she whispered. "He used the rope again."

"Who?" I asked, staring. I rubbed my eyes repeatedly, refusing to be part of her nightmare. Still, the marks did not leave.

She didn't answer; only pointed at her abdomen. "I hurt," she said in a voice from which all hope had long ago drained.

"Baby, I'm not going to let anyone hurt you," I told her. She stared at me blankly, then started to shake. "You're safe here," I told her, once, twice, and then again, repeating the words like a chant. The shaking increased until I thought she would shatter. Finally, she allowed me to cradle her, to pull her back under the covers, to smooth her hair and kiss her eyes and woo her back to sleep.

In the morning, I asked her if she remembered the dream. "The night is very black," she told me. "I remember nothing."

I remembered it, though. Something about it clung to me for days, like a cramp that wouldn't unfold. Then it struck me—how similar that childlike terror had been to the night when I'd forced myself on her and found her crying beneath me. It wasn't the cry only that I remembered; it was temperature. The child I'd found crying beneath me that night and the night of the first dream was as cold as an icicle; her body as white as the dead.

SMART LADY

The five-year-old is awake. Five, she calls herself. I don't know what to do. The child that Claw and I buried when the father died has come alive again, twitching and shaking in the arms of Gilly's husband.

Something is happening to Gilead. I fear for all of our lives. I have always been afraid for her; she breaks too easily. Little pieces shatter from her, leaving these half-people inside to carry on—Rita for sex, Five for pain, Claw in emergencies when fear paralyzes the rest of us, the twins for school. I catch glimpses of others, playing with ropes or dolls or trying to bring the cat back to life. They're like endlessly repeating plays, acted-out events and feelings trapped in separate niches, kept safely apart from the person that is Gilead.

Gilead knows nothing of us; I have always kept that information, all information, away from her skittish mind. But something is happening to her. Before, if any of the inside people got too close, she'd startle, go black. Then that person would come out, and Claw or I would hold Gilly until the danger had passed. Oh, I know it's not a perfect system. Rita's a real troublemaker, and the twins are so anxious to learn, they'll take anything in the house apart. It's safest to send them to the library—there's not much you can do to a book. But it all worked pretty well after the father died. Then Gilly decided to get married. And now, somehow, her husband or the marriage or Freddy or something has brought Five back to life. Gilly certainly can't bear that pain—that's why we put Five to sleep in the first place, and buried her when the father was buried.

I don't know what to do. For the first time, I am beginning to know fear.

NATHAN DEETERS

All this spring and summer there were nightmares, sometimes for several nights running, sometimes interspersed with days when Gilly's mood swung crazily high and low. The moods were almost physical in depth; her hazel eyes changing from green to brown, her body hunched or risen up tall and lean. She went on shopping sprees, bringing home clothes of such diverse styles—plain, dull dresses; sexy nightgowns, short-shorts, sun dresses that made her girlish and young. One minute her hair was wound tightly into a prim bun; the next minute it flowed softly over her shoulders. Even her handwriting was erratic. She had dozens of lists in her purse, on the refrigerator, tacked up on our closet door; some of them were in a perfect Palmer hand, others in a childish print, a few in a crinkly scrawl.

At night, I came to expect the dreams; they nearly always came in the first few minutes of deep sleep. I'd lie wrapped around her back or holding her in my arms, and wait for the deep breathing that signalled sleep. In a few minutes, she'd start to quiver and move, clawing at me, yelping in pain. Sometimes she jerked herself awake; other times I wakened her to stop the dreams. Always, she told of things too hideous to put down on virgin paper—vile sex acts, brutal beatings, things wrapped around her neck, being locked in closets and car trunks, dolls ripped apart with knives, a cat's head squashed by a man's boot as he shouted "Never tell! Never tell!"

At first I saw them simply as nightmares, the kind small children get when life on the outside seems so much larger and more demanding than what the inside has to offer. Something about the marriage—perhaps something about me—must be troubling her, I thought. But no matter how gentle I tried to be, how much I stuffed my irritations with her and her family or tiptoed around any obvious problem, the nightmares continued. Finally one night I erupted at her as she lay shaking in my arms. "Goddamn it, Gilly, you know I'd never hurt you!"

She stared at me with child eyes. "We know," she said in a round voice. "You're our safety man."

"I'm your husband," I said, still angry. "I don't do these things."

"No," she agreed. "That was the night-man. You're the safety man."

I stared at her, a gear finally clicking into place. "Who is the night-man?" I asked.

She shook her head. "Can't tell," she whispered.

"What did he look like?" I asked.

"Can't see," she said.

I paused, wondering if she was lying. "What does he sound like?" I asked.

"Loud," she returned. "And soft. Mean sometimes, and sometimes kind. Wanting. Angry. The worst times are angry."

I nodded, feeling quite lost—as if I'd been thrust into the role of psychiatrist with no training. How do doctors handle this? I wondered. Should I get Gilly a doctor?

"How big was he?" I asked.

"Very big. Very, very big. And strong. Big arms. Hairy."

I had a pretty good idea who this must be, but hated believing it. "Was it your father?" I asked.

"Can't say," she said quickly. "Can't see. Don't know."

"Do you think it might be?"

"Don't think. It's the night-man," she said, shutting her eyes and sinking quickly back to sleep.

◊ ◊ ◊

Two things were clear to me: Somehow, Gilly wanted me to hear these things, to know these things, to be there with her as she endured these things. I have no doubt of her need of me to usher her through these hellish visions, or of the comfort she took in my presence.

Or of the need I had to see her through them. That was the second part—I gradually came to see how much I treasured these experiences. I don't know why. Perhaps I was flattered by the enormous trust she was placing in me, telling me hideous things that, whatever their source, were clearly shattering some part of her soul. Or maybe it was that, in comforting her, in bringing out all the tenderness and comfort I could muster, I was somehow comforting myself. Or comforting my brother. My dead brother, the one I swallowed up.

CLAW

What the fuck am I supposed to do with these feelings? I wish to God Deeters would cut it out. He does help some, holding Five in his arms when the pain comes out. I siphon it off as fast as I can, but some of it's coming through to Gilly—she's starting to smell it, hear it. Soon she'll start to feel it.

The others are all feeling it now. They argue constantly, screaming, attacking each other, trying to get out, to kill Five, to kill the pain. I CAN'T HOLD THEM ALL. Doesn't he see that?

Maybe Rita's right—maybe the only solution is to kill Gilead. But can we kill *ourselves*? Or Deeters—maybe we should kill Deeters. What the fuck does he think he's doing? Gilead, oh my love, Gilead.

Yours,
Claw

GILEAD

There is something wrong with my eyes. Everything looks watery and far away, as if I am staring at the world through a distant sheen, a waterfall. It reminds me of those paintings with little dots, where the dots make the picture. They are beautiful, pastel. But my world is dark, pricked, broken. It is hard to see. Sometimes I see parts that my mind tells me are not there. Like the child my husband carries, still drags around on a chain. He is there, dead, ready for final burial. My husband turns to him, tells me fantastic things about him, tries to paint him with color and light. I think my husband has been siphoning off parts of himself for years, years, thinking it was going to the child. Thinking that the child carried his core. But the child is dead. The child must be truly buried.

NATHAN DEETERS

Sometimes I wonder how my brother would have handled Gilly. Would he have known, better than I, what to do? Would the successes I've painted into his life have armored him to handle this much pain? Or would he, like so many other successful people I've known, simply have dismissed her as one of the mad, the untouchables?

It seems somehow disloyal to carry these thoughts. But for the first time since I buried my brother, I'm starting to wonder about that successful path—a path I knew would have taken me far away from this depleted life I've led. Was it simply, as I suspect, a lack of courage on my part that stuck me in this webby life? Or was it a yearning for something that other path could not bring?

SMART LADY

Husband had a dream last night. We found him quietly weeping, a smear of tears rimming his eyes. I listened carefully, sending Rita to hold him close against her breasts as he told his tale.

In the dream, he said, he was on a journey, and stopped at a grocery store for food. There was a woman he identified only as the long-haired one, bending over the meat section, searching for something to eat. All of a sudden, he said, he saw that she was someone he knew quite well, though he couldn't name her. But he had mistaken her for a customer, and asked if she needed help finding anything. She turned to him and stroked his face sorrowfully, telling him what she needed was not there. He searched frantically around the store, trying to find anything that would hold her, meet her need. He wondered if he shouldn't check at home—if something was stored there that she needed. When he looked around, he realized that she'd gone. He checked all the other groceries in town, looking for her. He was going to tell her he could order the thing she needed, that he could get it in stock if she'd just tell him what it was. But he couldn't find her in the other stores.

Then for some reason, he decided to look for her in the park. He wandered around, searching behind trees and along the banks of a wide, wide river near the bridge. He thought he saw her ahead of him several times, but she'd disappear by the time he caught up. Finally he saw her resting by the riverbank in the shadow of the bridge. But when he caught up with her, he found that it was not the long-haired woman. It was Gilly. She was sobbing, holding herself open, her body. He looked inside, and found the thing the woman needed, beating in there, covered with blood.

Husband looked up at us as he finished telling this dream, like a lost child. "I don't even know what it was inside you," he said. "I just know that it's the thing I was missing."

"Take me," Rita whispered back to him, rolling him toward her and spreading herself for him. "Take it all. It's all for you; only for you."

He took her then, pushing himself inside—slowly at first, and then with quick, compulsive thrusts. Rita dug her fingernails into him, opening herself, inviting his surges, willing him deep inside her. Finally he cried out with relief and pain, heaving and sobbing in her arms.

But the arms had changed to that of another person, a stronger person. It was Gilly who held the husband, making her arms strong and gentle, cradling him until he was blessed by sleep.

GILEAD

Something is bothering my husband. I think it's me, the toxic part of me. He says I'm having nightmares again, asks me if I remember them. I don't remember—or I remember only on the edges, with the dream skating around the rim of memory, just out of reach. When I was a child and had nightmares, father had to lock me in the closet or tie me to the bed, they got so bad. I must have been very dangerous. Very bad. I was a very bad child.

My husband must know this now—how bad I am. And yet, there's something about him that makes me feel like a good person. Perhaps it's his own goodness. Perhaps it's because I love him so much. Love *can't* be bad, can it?

Chapter 12

August 1991

NATHAN

Something needs to be done. I must face it: my wife is ill, seriously ill. The stuff of these nightmares has got to get out—she's got to deal with them in the light of day. I'm convinced that something hideous happened to Gilead as a child, something that shattered her in some fundamental way. She is shattered, into pieces. Her moods are like pieces, pieces of people. She's like a lot of different people—the little girl, the sexpot, the practical one, the Vapor Woman. I never know who I'm dealing with—something I find vastly irritating. And depleting. She's exhausting to be around.

And those nightmares! My God, what kind of monster was her father? I can't believe it. But I do believe it—it's the only explanation that makes sense.

For one thing, it makes everything else fall into place. Like the countless quirks of behavior—the way she stuffs toilet paper into the bathroom keyhole when she takes a shower, as if she's afraid I'll peek through. The odd aversion to luggage (she made me lock the closet where I keep mine; refused to use a suitcase when we went to Rehoboth for a few days). The stuffed animals she keeps under the bed. The way she practically attacks me in bed at night, and then insists on dressing in the bathroom in the morning. The way she seems to forget all her math facts, and then suddenly can do percentages and long columns of figures in her head. And her reaction to rope.

Freddy pointed that one out to me, without explaining (no one in this family ever explains). They'd come to the store to pick up the car, and found me in the back room, working over my accounts. I keep rope there, of course—things must be tied in my business. I'd noticed before Gilly's aversion to that room, the silly excuses she puts up for not entering, the way she keeps her eyes down when she does come in. She was feigning interest in the chips stand when Freddy found me. I called to her to come in; I wanted her to see the splendid effect of her reworking the inventory system. She always seems more alert with Freddy; I thought perhaps I could renew her interest in the business. But she shook her head in the doorway, smiled and said, "We can't go in there." Then she turned, and left the store.

I looked at Freddy, hoping for some illumination. He provided one that holds more mystery than light. "It's the rope," he said, jerking his thumb toward the wall where it hung.

I looked. "What about it?" I asked.

He stared at me, puzzled. "She's scared of it."

"Why?" I asked. Specifics, that's what I need if I'm ever to help this girl.

"Cause of Pa," he said, then turned away.

"What about him?"

"Could we just have the keys?" Freddy said in a voice that sounded like it wanted to bite. "Please," he added, nastily.

That made me angry. "Perhaps I'll ask Gilly," I suggested.

And ducked. Freddy pulled himself up to his full five feet, nine inches, and came at me. "Don't you ever mention rope around her, you understand?"

"No, I don't understand," I told him. I'd moved around the desk by this time—cowardly, I suppose, but I doubted I could take the boy, he was so full of rage. "I believe you, but I don't understand."

"Just leave her alone." His fists were up, close to his chest.

"Freddy, she's my wife. I want to help. But I can't unless someone tells me what's going on."

He stared at me, his rage oozing into confusion. The fists had become the tightly held hands of a little boy, I noticed. He started to stammer, so quietly I could barely hear.

"Something bad," he began, and then dropped his hands and his head, "happened."

I waited. "To Gilly," I suggested. He nodded limply. "With a rope?" I asked. "And your father?"

He nodded.

"You mean your father tied her up?"

"Yes," he admitted. "No," he added. "Worse. Gilly and I...." He stiffened, and looked at me with panicky eyes. "Just don't hurt her, okay?"

"Of course I won't hurt her—I'm not a monster, you know," I began, but he grabbed the keys from the desk where I'd laid them, and jerked out the door before I could finish. "I'd never want to hurt her," I told the door as he left.

SMART LADY

Gilly is growing, changing, splintering and reforming. Each day she bounces crazily between despair and strength, like an atom out of control tearing through a universe of molecular possibilities. A little of Claw's strength adds on here, some of the twins knowledge there. A flicker of Rita's risk-taking flashes through from time to time.

But it's Five she's leaning towards most of the time, coming ever nearer to the pain and reality. I suspect she sees Five occasionally, growing mesmerized by the message she brings her of her own past. But then Gilly veers off at the last second, unable to touch the white-ice pain that is Five.

The nightmares help her to touch it, through the drugged state of narcoleptic distortion. She tells the husband she remembers nothing of the nightmares, refuses to discuss them. But something of the night clings to her, brings her to her knees at sharp moments throughout the day. If too much gets through, she'll collapse. How much—this is what I don't know, must know—how much is too much?

NATHAN

Missy wasn't much help either, when I spoke with her about Gilly's state. "I'm afraid Gilly is ill," I told her at the store where she'd come, as usual, to solicit funds.

"Oh, how terrible!" she exclaimed in that phony voice. "Is it the flu, or just a cold?"

"Neither," I said. "I meant mentally ill."

"Pardon me?" She looked mock-shocked.

"Gilly seems to have some form of mental illness," I said in as controlled a voice as I could manage.

"Oh, no, I'm sure you're mistaken. There is no madness among the Grasons," she said.

I saw just the opposite, but said nothing. "She has nightmares," I informed her.

"Oh, those. Well, no wonder you're concerned. Yes, they can be quite disturbing, n'est-ce pas? So difficult to sleep, with all that screaming. Why, you must be plain worn out, poor man."

"It's not my sleep I'm concerned about," I said, stiffly. "It's Gilly's. The nightmares are quite hideous. And they all seem to concern your fa…"

"Well, they're nothing to worry about, I'm sure," Missy told me. "She's had them for simply ages. Now, the real reason I'm here is…"

"Has she ever seen a doctor?"

"A doctor? Oh, my, yes, of course. There have been oodles of doctors. Nothing we can do about it, but just accept it, I'm afraid. Mr. Deeters, I must talk with you about…"

"A psychiatrist?"

"Well, yes, I believe the last doctor may have been a psychiatrist, or psychologist, or some such brain person. Nothing wrong with her brain, of course—that was thoroughly tested. Actually, Gilly's quite bright. Used to astonish her teachers."

"What was his name?"

"The teachers? Well, there were quite a few of them, I don't remember them all."

"I meant the doctor," I said with the last shred of patience I had left.

"The doctor? What was his name—Madison? Madsen? Matthews? Oh, dear, I'm afraid my memory isn't…"

"Is it written down somewhere? Or would your mother remember? Or Freddy?"

"I have no idea. Oh, Mr. Deeters, I'm afraid I'm so worried about our little family, I simply can't concentrate on something so long ago. Please, I appeal to you. I need your manly advice on a question of great importance."

Which was money, of course. Missy had some idea that she could drive the VW bus to do my pickups, for a spare $1000 per month. When I refused, she broke out in copious crocodile tears, and started in on a tale of how mean her aunt was and how difficult it was to manage with her mother and their poor pension, etc., ad nauseum.

"What happened to the insurance?" I asked. Again.

"Insurance?" she asked.

"You told me your father had insurance," I reminded her.

"Oh, yes, well. But they wouldn't pay," she said. As she took her next breath before plunging back into her woe tale, I said,

"Why not?"

"The circumstances of his death prevented it. Honestly, I thought I'd already explained this."

"What circumstances?"

Now Missy was mock-enraged. "I'm not going to stand here and talk about our family's tragedy in full view of the entire town," she said. Actually, she was standing in the back room. The rope didn't bother her, I'd noticed.

I tried to figure out how the circumstances of anyone's death would prevent insurance, and only came to one conclusion. "Did he kill himself?" I asked.

"That was never proved," she said. "There was no note."

"So what did happen?" I asked.

"Ask Gilly. But don't expect us to take her back when you do."

"Just what does that mean?"

"Nothing," Missy said, implying Everything. "I just hope you're insured. Are you?"

"Of course I'm insured," I told her angrily. "But what does that have to do with…"

But she'd already started through the door. She turned around, and jerked her thumb toward the rope. "I'd keep her away from that, if I were you," she said.

GILEAD

I think I'm losing my mind. Life has always seemed harder for me than it appears to be for most people. Mother says it's because I was born fragile, but does that really explain it? Most people get up, make their beds, put on their shoes without thinking, it seems. Each one of these things has always been a challenge to me, something I do by gritting my teeth and telling myself I must. And I have. I have. Didn't I get good grades in school? That was so long ago; I can't imagine how I did it. Didn't I win a prize for math? I remember looking at it. Father had it framed in the living room. He was proud of me, before he left. Or died. Sometimes I think that father died. Everytime I think that, I get dizzy, panicky. I want to run away. Where would I go?

I'm starting to see something out of the corner of my eye. A little girl. She squats there in unlikely corners, turning up under the kitchen table, inside closets, peering around the sofa as I turn the pages of a book. She's covered with filth, excrement. Her hair is matted. She looks so lost. I long to go to her, but she looks so repulsive. Plus, she's not there, not really. She can't really be there. I must be losing my mind.

NATHAN

Did her father use a rope on Gilly? He must have. That must be it.

Or did Gilly use a rope on her father?

Chapter 13

September 1991

SMART LADY

Everything is shaking. The very structure has become unloosed; I don't know how much longer Claw and I can hold it together. If the inside collapses, what will we do? We will all be crushed in here if something's not done. And Gilly will break off from us—a small sliver of a person, with no one to prop her up.

Claw was all for telling the husband, shoving him into a corner and shouting at him about the pit, the ceiling, the way everything was starting to collapse into itself. I squeezed out ahead of Claw, hoping to reason with the husband. But he finds our world so alien, I'm not sure how much got through.

"All this has to stop," I told him as he lay propped against the pillows on the bed, still stroking Gilly's body. "Everything is leaking. Things are falling down. We can't keep it up anymore."

He stared at Us in puzzled discomfort. Finally he asked, "What do you mean, We?"

Could he really not know, after all these months? The question seemed to evoke a feeling in me. Anger. Claw must be standing at my back, ready to throw the knife. I have no feelings, of course. It's not possible to do my work within the messy context of feelings. Claw must be getting more powerful, I thought. It was as if I could really feel that anger. I pushed it away.

"The brood," I told him as carefully as I could. This was a risk, I knew. What if he told Gilly? "Those that live inside."

"Are there many of you?" he asked in a voice made hoarse, sanded down by emotion. I wondered, idly, how people manage with the full cacaphony of emotions they must endure. No wonder they so often appeared deranged; it must be unbearable to feel everything you experience.

"Yes. Husband, I am telling you this in confidence. It's very important that Gilly not be told. Do I have your word on this?" The husband possesses something unknown in our family: Honor. It seemed the easiest thing to exploit.

He was not quick to give it over. "Why not?" he asked.

I sighed, feeling Rita's exasperation like a finger at my temple. "Because she would collapse," I told him. "She would remember what happened with the father, and collapse."

He nodded, looking puzzled and sad. I could feel Rita trying to reach the body's arms out to him, found I'd put fingers on his arm. I shoved the fingers back; there was no time for the luxury of comfort.

The husband had pulled his legs up to his chest, and was holding his head in his hands. I could feel Rita flailing around inside me. Five whispered that the dead brother, the one the husband continually drags alongside him, was starting to glow. Claw snarled "Fuck this" and left, much to my relief. I waited for reason to re-emerge. Finally his hands dropped from the husband's tired face. "I guess I knew—well, I knew, but I didn't know. I knew, but I didn't understand. I'm glad you told me." He smiled weakly. "I do want to help. Tell me what to do."

I told him all that I knew—about the pit where the pain was buried after each of us was created, the grave where we'd laid Five, our fear when he'd brought Five back to life, the jealousy Rita felt when he called for Gilly, the curiosity of the twins as they pored over his accounting system, his store, his books, his possessions. I left out a few things—Claw's murderous anger, the times I'd had to stop Rita from trying to kill both him and Gilly, the doctors we'd had to fool to escape institutionalization.

He treated it all in that odd analytic way of his, protecting himself by putting a notebook on his lap, asking questions, jotting down answers. He wanted to know a jillion things—about the angel who created us, where was He kept? How often did we see Him? What was the circumstance of each birth, how long had we lived, how did we each come out and when. He made charts, geneologies, histories in the hours we talked; asked me to draw pictures of the pit, the layers, the door we use to enter and leave.

But for all of his blatant fascination, I felt he'd blocked off the central point of the discussion. I tried to bring him back to the subject of collapse with each set of questions. "The structure is shaking," I explained as he asked for structural details. "We're leaking into each other," I said as he did biographies of each of us. I told him of the way I was jarred by surprising anger; the way the twins were starting to look at people through my eyes; the way Rita's desires were leaking into Gilly.

"You mean sexual desires?" he asked, looking up.

"Yes," I nodded. "Gilly is there at the beginning now, sometimes." He looked puzzled. "When you begin lovemaking," I added.

"You mean I've never made love to Gilly?" he asked, his eyes widening.

"Of course not," I said, a little sharply. "Gilly is a virgin."

The statement seemed to hit him with considerable impact. "Is she frightened of me?" he asked.

"She's frightened of sex, as all young girls are," I told him.

"I see," he said, completely distracted. "So perhaps if I was very gentle with her," he began, but I'd had enough of this conversation. Gilly's budding sexual desires were the very last thing we needed to worry about.

"Husband, we must deal with the structure first. The structure is collapsing. You must help us."

He sighed, and turned his attention to the notebook. Sunrise was starting to soften the room, I noticed. We must have been at this for hours. "When did things first start to collapse?" he asked.

I was exhausted by then, and missed the significance of the question. I'm rarely out this long; it's difficult to work the body for any length of time, and I longed to go back into my closet. And time questions are especially difficult; we live outside of time, none of us has much understanding of a thing like that. It changes continually, will not be pinned down. "I'm not sure," I said, rubbing the body's eyes. "Perhaps I could think about it, and talk to you later."

But his eyes, gleaming like an archeologist who's just discovered an intact tomb, pressed on. "Was it collapsing before the marriage?" he asked.

"No," I said. The structure was solid before the marriage.

"Did you notice it at the wedding?"

I hadn't gone to the wedding—a protest, I suppose. "No," I told him. Then it came to me: "Five. It was when you brought Five back to life."

And with that, I submerged.

NATHAN

I watched her eyes close and sink; watched the body shudder. Then there was a slow series of eye blinks. I've seen this before, I thought. This has been happening all along.

The eyes that opened looked frightened, confused. Haunted. "Gilead?" I asked.

She looked at me and smiled, a shy, young-girl smile. Her hand went to my unshaved face. I kissed her hand and then her mouth, as gently as I could. Her eyes closed, started to blink. "I want to make love to you," I told her softly. "Gilead. My wife. I want to make love to my wife." The eyes opened and gave me a narrow, calculated look, then closed. More blinks. The eyelids opened again to frightened eyes. "We'll go slowly," I told her, "and stop whenever you want." I moved my hands gently up and down her back. "I'm not going to force you. I'm just going to love you. All right?" She nodded, gasping a little.

And so I started to seduce my wife, a slow process that took several nights of starts and stops and building trusts. My marriage was consummated on a soft autumn evening, a year after our vows were spoken, when she finally let me know with a shy nod that she was willing to let me enter her. "Stay with me, Gilly," I whispered to her, moving as slowly as I dared. "Open your eyes, darling, and look at me. I'm loving you now, as a man loves a woman." I thrust into her a little more quickly, feeling her soften slightly beneath me. "As a husband loves a wife. Stay with me."

It took three more nights of trying to bring her to orgasm, her eyes widening in amazement as her sweet cries reached up the octaves. I lost control in the deliciousness of that moment, wrapping myself around her shuddering body and thrusting myself to an orgasm that seemed almost like an afterthought. As I finished, I found that I was crying, the tears spilling over the rims by their own volition. I felt so happy, and strangely amused. I, who had been so dry, gushing tears—who would have thought it possible?

Eventually the tears stopped, and I was left with a deep and tired joy. We lay there entwined, and fell gently into a long and innocent sleep.

Chapter 14

October 5, 1991

SALLY

      Diet Manuscript

 Idea for new-type diet based on sunspots. Look for sunspot article clipped from National Inquiry (check in hankie drawer—I'm sure I saved it) about how moods are affected by changes in sunspot activity. Lead: "Is this you? Most days, you're a sensible eater. You keep yourself up-to-date on nutrition, eat lots of fruits and vegetables, limit your snacks and keep yourself away from foods that are too rich or salty.

 "But some days—and even at certain periods of most days—your body just seems to cry out for cakes and cookies, potato chips and sour cream. You find yourself inexorably drawn to the refrigerator or the vending machine, stuffing these illegal foods rapidly into your mouth. Is this, as some experts would have us believe, a psychological problem?

 "No! According to the latest study by the renowned Dr. (check article), the element resonsible for this strange, compelling need to eat rich or salty foods is not you—but sunspots!"

 Need to find chart that predicts periods of intense sunspot activity, to warn readers. Recommend that they limit themselves to certain sunspot foods during these periods, e.g. prunes, black-eyed peas, raisins, black beans, etc.

 Idea: Is it sunspots that rule Gilly? She's been so strange lately. Her new-found chattiness is a delight—even sister has noticed it. Of course, I'm not sure about that scheme she has for going to college to take accounting courses. I know Missy has some concerns about the stress it will place on her. And I'm concerned that she might learn more than her husband (she'll have him thinking she's smarter than he is, and the first thing you know she'll be out on the street). But Gilly says Mr. Deeters is all in favor of it—that it was his suggestion in the first place. Sister says that Mr. Deeters wouldn't mind even if Gilly was better at accounting—says that men nowadays appreciate office help from their wives. How Sister would happen to know that is beyond me. She claims to pick up all kinds of things through her church prayer group, but I think they're a mighty peculiar bunch of people. Besides, Mr. Deeters isn't Baptist.

Idea: Perhaps I could get the famous scientist in the National Inquiry article to write an introduction to my sunspot diet. That would lend it a certain authenticity. Should I write to him first, or contact the publisher?

Idea: Perhaps sunspots are also responsible for extreme changes in mood. Gilly is like a pendulum these days, rushing off in that Volvo to see Freddy in Annapolis, and then burying herself at home with her books. One minute she seems happy to see me, asking me about my Tarot readings and my publishing success (two hints and a recipe already this year! And it's only October!). Then she turns for the door and makes some very rude wisecrack about growing up in a crazy family. As if we were the ones that were crazy! If I hadn't vowed never to mention the hospital again, I'd have a thing or two to say to that young lady!

She actually had the nerve to ask me about what happened to Rod. I told her, of course, that I didn't want to discuss it.

"But why not, Mama?" she asked.

"I see no need for that kind of talk," I told her, and turned toward the television.

"I do. And my husband does," she said.

"Your husband!" I said before I could stop myself. "Gilly, you're not discussing this with Mr. Deeters, are you?"

She looked down. Oh, I knew she was guilty, all right. "You must never, never tell Mr. Deeters."

"But why not, Mama?" she said, crying. I know that old ploy—as if she had anything to cry about.

"Because it's none of his business, that's why."

"Mama, I'm having nightmares again," she told me.

Not again, I thought. Dear God, not again. "How bad are they?" I asked, afraid to know.

"They wake me up," she said.

I panicked a bit, and suggested we go get Missy, who was making something yummy in the kitchen. But Gilly held my hand, and wouldn't let me go. "I don't want Missy to know, Mama," she told me.

"But why not?" I asked. "Missy's your sister, your twin. Surely she should know."

"Missy's never been married," she said.

Then I understood. "Oh, my poor baby," I said. "Has that bad man been hurting you?"

She denied it, of course—I expected my daughter to be loyal to her husband. But I knew at once what was going on. "Move out of the bedroom," I told her, whispering so no one would hear us. "Tell him you're ill. Tell him you can't sleep with his snoring. Tell him anything—you're much too fragile, you can't be expected to bear that kind of...."

"Mama, you don't understand. It's not my husband. I love my husband; he's very kind to me. It's just, there are things I need to know about, about...."

"S-E-X?" I whispered.

"No. Yes. About father. About father and sex."

I rose up and left, of course. I'm certainly not going to discuss my husband's sex life with my daughter. The very thought of it!

Question: Should I send the diet first to Ladies Home Companion, and then spin-off a book? Perhaps it would be picked up by Reader's Analog! Or should I sell the book first, and then approach magazines to do a shorter version?

Question: Just how much has Gilly told Mr. Deeters? Not that we have anything to be ashamed of. But Gilly has no business discussing family affairs with him, even if he is her husband.

Should I speak with Mr. Deeters, explain that Gilly often exaggerates things? I don't want him believing that we've been anything but loving to Gilly. Didn't Rod always spoil her, buying her all those dolls and that awful cat? Of course he had a right to expect affection in return. But the very idea that there was anything unseemly about it—well, Gilly's just lying. She always was a liar. Should I speak with Mr. Deeters?

I just don't know.

Chapter 15

October 17, 1991

FIVE

I talked to the man tonight. I've talked to him before, but he didn't know I'm me. He thinks we're all Gilly. But Smart Lady told him about us. Now he knows. Now he asks.

"Who are you?" he asked, right after I woke up. I had a bad nightmare. About the night man. I have them a lot. Usually I just snuggle with the man. He doesn't hurt us. His chest is furry. He doesn't get mad if I suck my thumb. Now he scared me, asking, who are you. I thought he'd be mad.

Just me, I told him.

"Which one are you?" he asked. He knew I wasn't Gilly. I just snuggled closer, and put my hand over my face so he wouldn't see. "You're little, aren't you?" he asked. His voice is gentle. He wasn't mad. "How old are you?" I showed him fingers. I'm all the fingers on one hand, I think. Sometimes I look at those fingers. They're ENORMOUS! They're so BIG! And they don't look like mine. The whole hand is wrong, so long and skinny. With rings. Real rings, not drugstore rings. My body is much bigger, too, with really big feet and almost no tummy. It's real strange. If I close my eyes, it all goes away. Then I go back to being me.

"You're Five?" he asked. I nodded. "I've met you before, haven't I?" he asked. Uh oh, he knows. "Yes, I remember you," he said. "You're the one who likes my chest hair." I let go, like it was hot. "No, no—that's all right. I don't mind," he said. He was still holding me. "I want to help you all, honey," he said. "I want to help you get better. Can you tell me about the nightmare?"

I shut my eyes. "The night-man," I told him.

"Him again," the man said, and sighed. "What was he doing this time?"

He sounded terribly sad. I kept my eyes shut, and saw. And smelled. And remembered. Don't tell anyone. Dirty little girl. Dirty, dirty, dirty. "Dirty," I told him.

"He was doing something dirty?" the man asked. He was stroking my hair. I didn't know how he could stand it. Couldn't he tell I was covered with poop?

"I'm dirty," I told him. Everywhere. The poop is everywhere. Couldn't he smell it?

"Is that what he told you?" the man said. Couldn't he see? Couldn't he tell? I pulled back from him, showed him my hands.

"All dirty," I said.

"No, honey, you're not dirty," he told me. "The man just told you that. It's not true."

"IS true!" I told him. "Look! Poop! All over everywhere!"

"No, sweetie..."

"Everywhere! Everywhere! He put it everywhere! Look! Look! Look!"

NATHAN

She was screaming, hysterical. Convinced she was covered in excrement. I saw no way around her delusion—for her, it was obviously real. So I did what I could. I took her to the bathroom, ran the tub, removed her nightgown, and bathed her, head to toe. With each gentle scrub, each stroke of the washcloth, each cleansing rinse, I repeated what I knew to be true—she wasn't dirty, she wasn't bad. It was the night-man who had told her these things, I said. He was the dirty one. He was the bad one. He had hurt his little girl, when he should have been protecting her, loving her, guiding her. She calmed down considerably once I got her into the tub, giving out only occasionally with muffled sobs—more hiccups than tears. Finally I got her out and dried her off in terrycloth. She turned and pulled the plug. Together, we watched the water follow its gravitational pull down the drain. It became a kind of ceremony. It was clear she intended to stay until the last drop had disappeared. I stood there beside her, unsure as to what to do next. She must have felt my discomfort, for she took my hand. Then, as the last of the water finally gurgled its way down the drain, she turned to me and said, "all gone."

"The dirtiness is all gone," I assured her. "You're all clean now." She smiled at me, a kind of loopy, loving smile. "You're a clean little girl," I told her. Her lower lip tucked tentatively under her front teeth, and she stared at me expectantly. I wasn't sure what to do next. "You're a good little girl," I told her. She grinned at that, a bubble-shaped smile. I wanted to hug her, but was unsure how much physical contact she could stand at this point. So I patted her back rather tentatively. She showed no such restraint, but flung herself into my arms, there beside the porcelain basin.

"You made me ALL clean," she said.

"You always were clean," I answered, attempting again to show her the truth. "It was that bad man who made you feel that you were...."

"You made me ALL clean," she insisted.

"You're all clean now," I agreed. "And ready for sleep," I added. I pulled her to the bedroom, tucked her into her side of the bed, and crept carefully into my side.

The clock read 2:12 a.m. It was destined to ring in 3½ hours. How many more of these nightmares can there be? Something must be done.

I lay awake for the next hour, wondering whether I should notify someone—a psychiatrist, the county mental health board. But what if they decide to stick her in an institution? Or refuse to believe her? What if the word gets out that my wife has gone mad?

She thinks she's all clean, I remembered, smiling. With a simple bath. What could really cleanse her, once and for all, of these nightmares? Maybe if I confronted her, forced her to see the truth about her father....

Something must be done.

Chapter 16

October 18, 1991

MISSY

Disaster again! Auntie's phoned the police! And all over some trifle. I was simply trying to entertain her guests, who were surely only numbing their minds with all that talk of the new minister and the choir director's choices and the sales at Leggett's. Far better that they should hear nobler things, such as the joys and sorrows of a fictional life and the desperate dramas of an author's (my mother's) life. Auntie was lying when she said I was drunk. True, I do have a mild affection for bourbon, but I'm certainly not a tippler—not before 3:00, anyway, and only one drink at lunch.

Then she got on that old saw-horse about money. I admit my patience is wearing thin. I explained for the umpteenth time about the huge sums soap opera writers get, and how much All My Sorrows will pay after I get onto their regular staff as a correspondent. It's true, their response to my first script was less than enthusiastic ("Not for us" was not particularly illuminating), but the revision I sent last week is bound to knock their socks off.

I went to my room after this unpleasant discussion, only to be hauled down again to face a blue-uniformed brainless booby asking mother and me to leave the bosom of our family. We phoned Mr. Deeters, of course (there's no point in phoning Gilly—she won't pick up the bloody thing), but that cold, heartless man refused to take us in, even for a night. And I couldn't locate Freddy; it's just like the boy to be absent in our hour of need.

So I did what I could. I struck a deal with Auntie that we'd be out by the end of the month, and told her I'd look for apartments the very next day. She handed me the paper and said, Start now. The brute. I took it and headed off to my room, to write this saving chapter. She must see that my nerves are far too jangled to deal with anything as hideous as finding an apartment.

Well, this is it. Mr. Deeters will simply have to go. It's time for the seed I planted months ago in Gilly to come to fruition. Actually, I'm amazed it hasn't happened before now, the way she's been acting, all full of herself and snippy. Gilead has a funny mind. Parts of her seem incapable of the smallest act. But that's only a front. Parts of her are capable of anything, absolutely anything. I know; I'm her twin. Other families have skeletons in their closet; our family has Gilead—a living closet where our hopes and hatreds all are housed. Plant a seed inside and it ferments, mutating in the hothouse of rage into something hideous and terminal.

This time, it won't be the rope. Father's suicide did far more harm than good, I realize now. This time, it must be something even an insurance agent can see as an Act of God. An accident, perhaps.

Chapter 17

Friday, October 18, 1991

GILEAD

I had a dream, I told him. I had a dream about my father, my dead father. In the dream, I remembered that father was dead.

Yes, he told me, your father is dead.

I had a dream that I wanted to tell him something about my father. I was rising up out of the bed to tell him. These are the words I said: My father hurt me.

With words, or physically? he asked in the dream.

But then a corpse—I realized I was lying on the corpse—the corpse put its hands around my throat, pulled at me, pushed on my throat as I tried to answer. I was choking, trying to get the words out before all thought was strangled. This is all I could answer: Not with words. *Not with words.*

FREDDY

I was working on a 1982 Saab when they said I had a phone call. Figured it was one of my customers or Missy with one of her goddamn harangues about money. I barely recognized Gilly—can't imagine how she got this number. Gilly hasn't used the phone in a good five years.

"Freddy?" she asks. I'm thinking, who's this? "Is father dead?"

Sweet Jesus, I thought. Holy shit. "Where are you, sweetheart?" I could hear traffic in the background. She must have been in a phone booth somewhere. There was no answer. "Are you still in Cambridge?"

Gilly started to cry. "He's dead, isn't he?" she whispered.

"Yes, sweetie, he's dead. You're safe now." Where the hell was Deeters? "You want me to come?" More crying. "Look, why don't I come get you. We'll go get a beer or something, okay? Just tell me where you are."

"I don't know," she says. "I can only see rope. Freddy, tell my husband...."

Jesus, I thought. Sweet Jesus. Sweet Jesus.

"Tell my husband it's not his fault. His brother. Tell him, it wouldn't have made any difference if his brother had lived. Tell him that he's a whole person. Who I love. That I love the whole person."

"Gilly, let me speak to Smart Lady. You gotta let me speak to Smart Lady now. Come on, baby, let me speak to...." but then, the phone went dead.

MR. DEETERS

I can't find Gilly. It's been three hours since the argument; an hour since Freddy called and told me about the rope.

I told Freddy very few details about the quarrel. In fact, I've told very few details about Gilly to anyone. I debated bringing her to Dr. Langley for an exam, but was frankly frightened by what might happen with such exposure. He's famous in town for patching up emotional women with a pat on the head and a prescription for Prozac; something more than that is clearly called for here. But he could set the psychiatric gears in motion, a mechanism that leads directly to state institutionalization or (lately) heavy drugging, neither of which look like solutions.

So I compromised, speaking about Gilly to Father Benson, her favorite priest at church. But he completely misinterpreted my lament; started telling me how the first two years of marriage were the hardest, how all his parishoners gradually learned to live with their partner's inability to lower the toilet seat or properly squeeze the toothpaste tube or adjust to their spouse's temperature preference.

I listened to this list of trivial trials, and started to get furious with him, with all of us. Oh, I know these people—my customers, most of them—whose lives seem to skitter from one inconsequential event to the next. Watching them, day in and day out, I've seen how people allow their real selves, their pain, their grief, the losses that drain their lives, to be swallowed up, subsumed, reduced to the pockmarks of trivialities that rule their days. And once ruled mine.

But Gilly has opened a door into herself and let me in, shown me her pain like a long fingernail screaming down a chalkboard. And I, who once thought I had neither feelings nor memories, who was left only with memories of memories, memories of feelings, entered her world with horror, with revulsion—and with fascination. This is real, I thought. This is what raw, close, unillusioned reality feels like.

It's one thing to hear, to witness another's pain. It's something else entirely to make them feel it. I never should have insisted that she feel it. I never should have pushed her this far. I thought, in my protected state as witness, that by discussing her father in the cold light of day she could be made to deal with her past openly. That it would stop sending its earthquake tremors through her at night. That some of this pain would be allowed to escape, instead of recycling itself endlessly through her, charring all that it touched. Even when I saw the effect it had, of telling her that her father was dead, I pressed on.

God, I do believe, forgives the unrighteous when they come to repentence. But God should spare no mercy on the self-righteous, on the supreme egotism that lets us think we know what's best for any of His creatures. Dear God, what have I done?

◇ ◇ ◇

My wife protected herself. She did it by turning on me, attacking me over my brother.

"What about my brother?" I demanded, completely distracted. Her jaw set; she was stamped in silence. "Come on, out with it—what do you know about my brother." Nothing.

I was furious. I was furious, and I hit her. Oh, God, why did I do that?

She stared back at me in rage, the red mark of my hand still on her face. Her shoulders rolled up; she seemed to grow. Her tiny hands knotted into fists. A voice that was not hers—a low voice, a man's voice—rolled out of her. "Your brother is fucking dead, that's what I know. He's dead, he died, he was never born. It's all you, only you. That's all there is. That's all there ever was. Your mother didn't leave your brother; she left you. Your father didn't squash your brother down; you didn't stand up. You understand me?"

"I know that!" I said, rising up in the full fury of my self-righteous delusion. "I'm perfectly capable of facing the truth. But I also know that none of those things would have happened if he'd lived."

"But he didn't live."

"No, he didn't live. I know that. I can deal with that. You're not shocking me."

"But you think you killed him."

I rose, intending to hit him. Her. I decided instead to get a drink. I was afraid of what might happen. I left the room, went to the kitchen. I could feel poison pumping through me. I poured two fingers of vodka into a glass; downed it. I poured more. I needed to feel the click, that moment of relief when real feelings retreated. I heard something in the living room, a thud. I poured a third glass, took a sip, glanced out the kitchen window. Gilly was walking toward the road. She was carrying a rope.

FREDDY

I got to Auntie's house less than an hour after Gilly called. The place felt eerie, like a towel with one bloody fingerprint. Nobody seemed to be home. Auntie's usually gone—she goes off with her widows' group a lot during the week. And I supposed Missy was out trying to drum up money or look for an apartment or, who knows, even interview for a job (God help the office that gets her). Mother's soap operas were on, but she was nowhere around. I peeked into her bedroom, and was about to leave when I heard a thumping in the closet.

When I opened it up, there was mother, bound and gagged. For a split second, I thought father had somehow resurrected himself and hunted us down. Then my primary job of sweeper went into gear—I untied mother, pulled off the gag, and got an earful. Gilly had been there "hours and hours" earlier, and had gone stark raving mad, she said. She'd said the "vilest things about your poor, dear father," shaking mother and putting her face in front of mother's and pulling mother's hands off her ears when she'd refused to listen. Finally, when mother excused herself with a headache, Gilly had followed her into the bedroom with the rope, dragged her to the closet, tied her up, and "left me practically for dead. I've been in here for simply hours, Freddy. You have no idea how frightened I've been! Thank God you came."

I stared at the rope that had bound her. "So now you know how it feels," I said.

"I think we should call the police," mother said. "We can't have that girl out there on the streets. God knows what she'll do next. Freddy, are you listening to me?"

"Do you know how it feels now, Ma? Being tied up in the closet—do you know how it feels?" I was shouting into her little piggy unseeing eyes.

"Freddy, whatever are you talking about? Are you ill?"

"Do you know what it was like for Gilly in that closet? Do you know what it was like for Gilly on that bed?"

"I won't stand here and listen to this," she said, turning her tiny fat feet towards the telephone. "Has the whole world gone mad? I'm phoning Mr. Deeters."

"She's left Deeters," I told her.

"What? Oh, no, Gilly would never do that. Where would she go?"

That's when I knew. The bridge. She'd go to the bridge.

"Freddy, I'm talking to you," Mother said in that insidious, whiney voice. "Should we call the police? I think you should do it, don't you?"

I turned to her, allowed myself to see her in all her fat, uncaring, self-centered glory. "No, I don't," I told her, grabbing her overstuffed hand and pulling her back to the closet. I pushed her in, and locked the door.

NATHAN

There's something wrong with the car. When Freddy showed up half-an-hour ago with a tale about Gilly heading for the bridge, I suggested that we take off in the Volvo and see if we could catch up with her. Freddy believes she's hitchhiking, which seems entirely out of character to me. Freddy says she did it in her adolescence.

But there's something wrong with the accelerator; I couldn't seem to get it to find a gear. And of course Triple Z is taking its own sweet time about getting here with the tow truck. I suggested that Freddy run back and get his mother's bus, but he tells me it's not at home—Missy must have it. He ran back to get his motorbike; told me he'd meet me at the bridge.

I've been racking my brain, trying to think of someone, anyone, from whom I could borrow a car. Someone in the book discussion group? Someone from church? They'd all think it very odd, want an explanation. I cannot think of even a reasonable lie to cover my urgency. How did I ever let my life get this friendless?

I keep thinking about Gilly's statement—how she loves the whole man. Does she really know me so little? My life is anything but whole. I have gone dry, living it. I have let myself become a half-man, covering up by assigning all real life to my brother, my unborn brother. I can see that now.

And I can see, too, that Gilly has become crazed as china is crazed, fractured into jagged pieces. But the pieces are still there to fit together, a puzzle, a whole picture. By examining each of those sharp and dangerous pieces, she's started to put herself back together.

Is this what life does to us? Are we all fractured by it, grown jagged at the edges?

I must let her know. I must get to her, tell her—what? That I love her. That it doesn't matter if she does or does not think about her father's death. That she's the first person who's ever loved me for what I am, not for what I could be or for what they wanted me to be. That no matter how jagged the pieces of her become, I'll hold them. I'll hold them all.

Ah—the Triple Z truck. Perhaps the driver will know enough to be able to fix this wretched car. Freddy said he thought the bolt on the accelerator linkage was loose, whatever the hell that is. "But how would that happen?" I asked him, expecting some convoluted explanation that would wind up costing me hundreds.

"Not how, but who?" he said, obliquely, before running off.

I can't think about what that might mean. The Triple Z man has my hood open. Dear God, make it something simple. I must get to Gilead. Gilead, my love.

MISSY

Just when I, the author, felt this chapter lunging towards its natural end—when I'd gotten the last shoelaces tied and was ready to let the characters walk their literate path—the plot twisted a quarter-turn too far, and kept spiralling.

I'd spent most of this afternoon in a fine drinking establishment that's become a regular haunt for me. It's a perfectly respectable thing for a fictional character to do, I felt. By frequently favoring the establishment with my presence, I'd joined a long list of other authors—F. Scott Fitzgerald, Ernest Hemingway, Jack London, just to name a few—who found that liquor opened a direct line to their muse. This particular cafe has a number of refined gentlemen customers who, I've discovered, are willing to buy me a drink or two—indeed, a whole series of drinks—in exchange for scintillating conversation, something I get pathetically little of in my own home.

Enter Gilly, looking madder than a stirred-up hornet's nest. I must say her features had changed considerably since I visited with her this morning. I'd stopped by her house for a cup of tea, to plant the last seed that needed to grow for this plot to be neatly tied. You see, Mr. Deeters has taken to walking to the store, to leave his car at Gilly's disposal. That gave me ample opportunity to perform a small mechanical operation (Freddy isn't the only one with mechanical knowledge in our family). I had only to persuade that part of Gilly that sees things in black-and-white to provide Mr. Deeters with a reason to drive.

Gilly doesn't work by faints. Threats worked marvelously well on the girl until our father died; after that, all effect had to be carefully crafted through manipulation. Enhanced with liquor. I poured several fingers of vodka into the teapot, and opened up a tin of bourbon balls for the girl to sample. Then I started in on a long tale of Freddy's ills, the splendid effect her husband had on our brother's character, and a plea that she send him—alone—to our brother's rescue as quickly as possible.

She was by then in a docile and lethargic mood, so much so that I was unable to tell how far my words had penetrated. But she swallowed most of the tea, along with two bourbon balls, and nodded her head vigorously to my reminders by the door about Freddy. Of course, as we've seen, visual agreement on Gilly's part does not necessarily dip below the surface.

In the bar, to my great despair, it became apparent that all my words had fallen to the ground between us. She had become aggressive and frightening, speaking ill of our dear dead father and demanding to know why I hadn't stopped him. "From what?" I asked.

"From hurting me," she said.

"Don't be ridiculous, Gilly," I told her. "He never hurt you. Why, you were spoiled rotten by that man. Who got all the dolls? Who got to go with him on trips? Who got the new crayons, the special clothes, those huge lollipops after every trip?"

Gilly stared at me, puzzled and distressed. "But he hurt me," she said in a small voice. "I remember that he hurt me."

"He never did anything to you that you didn't deserve," I told her, plainly. "You were a morose, spoiled, rotten child. I'll admit that his punishments sometimes seemed extreme, but they ably fit the crimes."

"What crimes?" she asked, whispering. Then, louder, "what fucking crimes?"

"You were disobedient and ungrateful. All he wanted was a little affection, a little caring from the person he cared about most in the world. But you wouldn't give. You never cared for him the way I did. You never cared for anyone in your whole life, did you?"

The girl was crumbling in her seat. But then she rose up an inch or two and said, "I care for my husband."

Uh, oh, I thought. "Do you care about your brother?" She nodded limply. "Then I hope you've sent your husband to talk to Freddy." Nothing. "Have you?"

Dead silence. Then, weakly, "I forgot."

Jesus H. Christ, I thought, do I have to do everything myself? "I'll phone him," I said. "Excuse me."

"No, Missy, don't!" she said, pulling me back with those surprisingly strong arms. "You can't...that is, I've left him."

Here's my advice: Never invent characters with their own personalities, lest they stray far beyond your control. I intended for her natural wifely loathing of her husband to lead directly to his insurance policy; I never intended to face a divorce. "That's the most outrageous thing I've ever heard," I told her. "You must go home immediately. The Grasons do not divorce."

"I can't," she said. "I'm hurting him." That sounded good. "Everything in his life was small and contained before he met me; now it's open and running, like a fresh wound."

I was hoping for something a little more profound than that, but it would do for a start. Then I had a thought. "Sounds like you two need to talk this out," I told her. "But not at home—home can be a loaded place. I know a particularly nice restaurant on Kent Island near the bridge; that's a good out-of-the way place to go. It's within sight of the Bay Bridge, but there'll be no crossing over. And it's on the way to Annapolis; after you two talk, he can go directly to Freddy. I'll drop you off there, and then call your husband. How would that be?"

She was staring at the floor again, all personality drained from her. Finally, finally, she said something affirmative. It was: The bridge.

Once again, I thought the shoestrings were tied. I drove her to the restaurant, chatting amiably on the way about the pleasures of the Eastern shore, and seated her at a booth while I used the phone.

But when I called at Mr. Deeters' store, they said he hadn't come back from lunch. Calling at home produced his answering machine. I left messages in both places, and then had to decide between returning to the restaurant to keep a watch on Gilly, or driving back and looking for Mr. Deeters. I waited with Gilly for perhaps 20 minutes, but she'd gone mute again, with fear-filled eyes, and my patience, I must admit, wore out. I got her to promise to stay put (lots of head-bobbing), and took off to find Mr. Deeters myself.

It was easier than I thought it would be. He was standing impatiently on the shoulder of Rt. 50, watching as his car was hooked to a tow truck. Said there was something wrong with the accelerator (Note: If you want someone to die, you must narrow the variables).

Mr. Deeters seemed quite agitated about Gilly, saying he thought she'd taken off for the Bay Bridge. I was able to assure him that I knew exactly where she was; that she was waiting for him; and that I would be happy to drive him there in the bus. He looked rather dubious when I mentioned the bus but, necessity being the mother of courage, took the plunge and got in. Now I have 60 miles to figure out how to guarantee insurance money for my family for life.

FREDDY

Traffic was backed up for miles on the bridge, with everyone feeding onto the incoming side. I drove on the shoulder, got close enough to see the cops and the blockade and the fire truck and ambulance at the top of the outgoing side.

"What's going on?" I asked the cop who stopped me, signalling me to get back in line.

"Suicide," he said, disgust in his voice. "They're up there, trying to talk her down, with everyone slowing down to gawk. Gonna be tied up for hours. Good thing it ain't summer—beach traffic would be hell."

"What's she look like?" I asked.

"Come on, buddy, back in line. You'll see for yourself at the top of the bridge—if she ain't jumped yet."

Don't hit him, I told myself. Keep your hands on the bike, and don't hit him. "Is she tall, with sandy hair?" I asked.

He looked at me suspiciously. "Could be," he said slowly. "You know her?"

"Could be," I said, concentrating on not gunning the engine and running the bike into his balls. "She might be my sister," I admitted.

"Oh, yeah?" he said. Ever the cop. "Describe her, then."

I did, making it as general as possible. Gilly looks different, depending on who's out. But I guessed no one was close enough to check details like eye color.

The cop took notes. Then he asked for my I.D., stared at my license for awhile, and got on the radio and muttered cop talk to someone who spoke back in static. I let myself gun the engine a few times, just to calm down. "Okay, go on up—real slow, you understand? Suicides spook easily. And talk to Joe."

I nodded, and took off.

GILEAD

Somewhere inside me, a child is crying, with the other voices saying, Let go, let go.

Somewhere inside me, a child is dying, with her tiny voice saying, Hang on, hang on.

MR. DEETERS

Gilly was not in the restaurant, as I suspected. Missy knows something, but is not giving it away. She went to check the ladies' room, and took an extraordinary amount of time doing it. Then entered the restaurant through the front door and said she'd had a look around outside. She suggested that she stay at the restaurant in case Gilly returns, and gave me the keys to the bus so I could run over to Freddy's apartment in Annapolis. I asked her if she was sure she didn't want to come, but she said, in that loud way of hers, "oh, we never go on the bridge if we can avoid it. You go ahead; don't worry about us a bit." The royal we, I presume.

I got a shock when I pulled myself into the driver's seat. I turned around to put my cap on the backseat, and saw a box there full of papers. Curious, I picked up the top one. It seemed to be some sort of story, perhaps one of those endless stories Missy's always writing. What shocked me was a sentence I read, stuck somewhere in the middle of the page but leaping up to my eye. Deeters must die! it read. Deeters must die!

Shaken, I turned to drive the bus toward the bridge. First things first; I must get to Gilly. But I'm a little fearful about driving this bus. Second gear doesn't seem to exist. And the brakes aren't responding well.

FIVE

There is an old song playing in my head; I don't remember where it came from. Something Gilly used to sing as she rocked by the window. It says that the cost of freedom is death. Death.

Smart Lady says that I am that cost. I am what had to die for the rest of us to go on. And now, they want to bury me again—this time, forever.

No. No.

There is a man, a safety man. He'd hold me sometimes, when the pain came out. He'd hold me and rock me and tell me I was safe. There was a hole inside him where a baby used to be. I'd crawl in there, and stay safe. He made me all clean. But now, they want me to leave him.

No. No.

FREDDY

I figured they'd put me through umpteen more layers of bureaucracy before they'd let me up the ladder to talk to Gilly. But I just told them that was my sister, and they hustled me along. "We haven't been able to get close enough," Joe told me. "Everytime we move the ladder, she climbs higher on the cable. We're not even sure she can hear what we're saying, the wind's so bad up there."

Oh great, I thought. I'm scared to death of heights.

Every other rung going up that ladder, I stopped to look back and see what was going on. That's how I happened to see the family bus come reeling up the left-hand lane, crash through the orange triangles blocking the road, and careen toward the fire truck that held my ladder. I could see someone in the driver's seat—not Missy. Maybe Deeters? My God, I thought, as the bus bolted forward. He's going to kill me.

SMART LADY

They're all out of control in here. Rita's sure that the only decisive way to bury Five is to drop her headlong into the Chesapeake Bay, and she's got Claw believing her. The twins are no help—they're fascinated by the bridge and keep moving around, examining the construction. Gilly is completely depleted with all of us arguing like this—she only does what we tell her to anyway, and with all these mixed messages, she's gone stiff. Only Five, the one person I'd be glad to see go, seems determined to live.

I only manage; I don't cause. And if I just let the fingers stray from these wires, unwrap the legs from this giant erecter set piece, I'll never have to manage again.

Someone is calling my name. That's strange. I look over, and see the top of a giant ladder coming near me. Freddy is on the ladder, looking scared. What's he got to be scared about?

Then I see it—the family bus running like a bat out of hell toward the fire truck. The ladder is now resting on the cable we're clinging to. The bus looks like it's going to crash. Hold on, Five, hold on!

FIVE

I'm hanging on a rope, a smooth, huge rope. How did I get here? When I was just me, I used to play with my dolls under a fir tree. Then I got all dirty, and went inside. The next thing I knew, I was lying next to a furry man, telling him about the hurt. The man stroked me, and called me good. He made me all clean.

But just look at me! I'm trapped inside this big body. I keep staring at it. The fingers are all wrong. Wrong shape. Wrong size. The arms are all wrong. The feet are all wrong. And look at those big, big sneakers! They even have shoelaces. Who tied them?

Somewhere along the line, I lost my body. This body belongs to the big lady. I can't be me inside it. Where did my little body go?

Somewhere along the line, I got losted. I got losted.

There is no ground for me. How can I stand?

NATE

The last thing I remember is diving into the backseat of the bus. I pushed, then shoved on the brakes when I saw the orange triangles blocking the lane that led to my wife. There was no response. Police cars hemmed me on the right; the only thing standing between me and a sky-deep plunge into the waters of the Chesapeake Bay on the left was a concrete wall whose strength I did not wish to test. That left a fire truck in front of me, its ladder extended and occupied by some bony youth in a denim jacket, waving frantically with one arm.

I took my foot off the clutch, jerked up the emergency brake, and dove into the backseat in time to be hit with the box-turned-projectile. I found myself wondering if Missy's words would come true. Would I die? Would it make a difference?

Two fellows in white jimmied the side door open; one started dabbing at my head immediately while the other made loud mechanical noises. There was the sound of talking everywhere, much of it amplified; I couldn't seem to sort it out. The fellow kneeling over me with a cloth wanted information: my name, my address, the date. None of these things had any relevance anymore.

They pulled me out and carried me on a stretcher past the fire truck to an ambulance already occupied with an empurpled Freddy. "Deeters," he acknowledged.

"How'd you get here?" I asked.

"Fell on the fire hoses," he said. "Luck of the Grasons, huh?"

"Where's Gilly?" I asked him.

He shrugged. "Couldn't see," he said.

"Where's Gilly?" I demanded of the white-coat.

"You lie back, sir," he said, pulling straps over my legs. "We've got to get you to Annapolis."

My brother's remains lie in Annapolis, at a graveyard there. There was a time when I'd visit him regularly, staring at the tiny headstone, testing my ability to contain my life against all that the headstone symbolized.

None of that mattered anymore. "I need to see my wife," I said, forcing myself to sit up. Everything in my head screamed against the move; I pushed my hands to my head for support, and found bandages already bloodied.

"We'll call her from the hospital, sir," said Whitecoat. "Lie back."

"You don't understand—she's on the bridge. She's going to jump off the bridge," I explained.

That slowed him down. "What's her name?" he asked, his hand poised with the last strap.

I looked over at Freddy for help. "What name would she respond to?" I asked.

"Smart Lady," he suggested. "That's your best chance."

"I'd better go," I said, undoing the leg straps.

"Sir, no, you're in shock, you can't...."

I ignored him, and heaved myself out of the ambulance.

◊ ◊ ◊

I have always been frightened of heights. I have always been frightened of myself. Each rung on the ladder was agony, with the wind whipping around me and the bandages dripping blood onto my left eye. With my right eye only could I see my wife, clinging tenaciously to one silken strand of this spider's web, albino with fear, shaking, eying the water below her. It was the cold, white child I'd held through those incessant months when she opened and disgorged her painful memory dreams. It was the woman who'd forced me to see the dishonesty I'd used to enamel my own life. I clawed my way up to her, and opened my arms to receive her.

FIVE

The man who held me is calling for me now. His face is bloodied and his clothes are torn. He is in pain. He wants me. The man who brought me to life again wants me to go down with him. We must all go down.

SMART LADY

All of our memories are buried with him, and with Gilead. With Gilead, our mother.

Gilead, are you listening? We will bury ourselves in you. Will you take us out from time to time, hold us, cradle us, give us your love? We were safety for you; you became courage for us. We were the silent half of language; now you must speak. Speak for us, Gilead. Speak for all of us who live inside.

One, two, three…ten fingers removed. We are falling. There is no ground for us.

GILEAD

I found myself pulled onto a ladder, descending into the arms of my husband, my beloved. There was blood covering one of his eyes, and I could feel his arms shaking with effort. I shifted to take the burden of myself from him. And I told him, with words that I felt had been jammed into my mouth for years, awaiting release: "I think I might have killed my father."

"Glad to hear it," he said. Just that—four words.

He sagged a little, and I could see the effort of coming to me had been too much for him. I put my arms under his, to steady him. "I killed my brother," he said.

"No," I told him, "you just survived."

He looked at me, cocking his head and smiling strangely. "Yes," he agreed. "Yes. We both survived."

Together, we crawled down the ladder, and stood on the bridge.